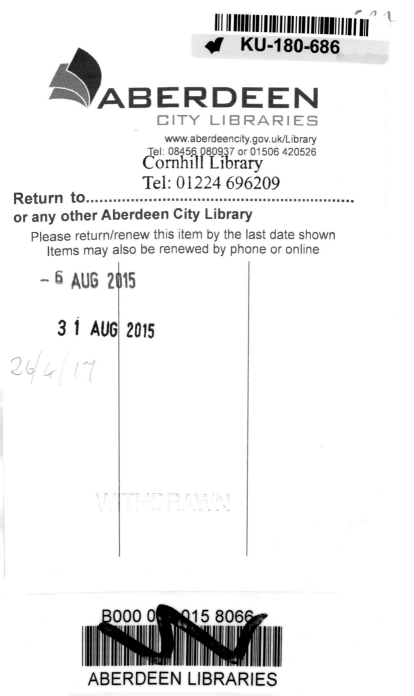

NEW YORK CITY DOCS

Hot-shot surgeons,
taking the world by storm...
by day and by night!

In the heart of New York City, four friends
sharing an apartment in Brooklyn are on their way
to becoming the best there is at the prestigious
West Manhattan Saints Hospital—and these
driven docs will let *nothing* stand in their way!

Meet Tessa, Kimberlyn, Holly and Sam as they
strive to save lives and become top-notch surgeons
in the Big Apple. Trained by world-class experts,
these young docs are the future—and they're taking
the medical world by storm.

But with all their time dedicated to patients,
late nights and long shifts, the last thing they expect
is to meet the loves of their lives!

For fast-paced drama and sizzling romance,
check out the
New York City Docs quartet:

Hot Doc from Her Past
Tina Beckett

Surgeons, Rivals...Lovers
Amalie Berlin

Falling at the Surgeon's Feet
Lucy Ryder

One Night in New York
Amy Ruttan

Available from August 2015!

Dear Reader,

For the last two books I've written I've had the good fortune of working with other talented authors to build a more complex world than you can normally cram into a short category-length book, and I have to say it's positively addictive. Not just the group brainstorming—which is terribly fun—but even better the knowing that I can send a half-coherent email in the middle of the night to double-check something without worrying the recipient will think me crazy.

Before this year I would never have guessed how much fun it would be to drag other author's characters into my book, and I must say I might have been spoiled by the experience...

I hope you enjoy Enzo and Kimberlyn's story, and I hope you will grab the other three in the *New York City Docs* quartet and follow the rest of the brownstone gang through their last year of surgical residency.

Wishing you health, love and happiness

Amalie

SURGEONS, RIVALS...LOVERS

BY
AMALIE BERLIN

MILLS
&
BOON

First published in Great Britain 2015
by Mills & Boon, an imprint of Harlequin (UK) Limited,
Eton House, 18-24 Paradise Road, Richmond, Surrey, TW9 1SR

© 2015 Amalie Berlin

ISBN: 978-0-263-25861-5

Harlequin (UK) Limited's policy is to use papers that are natural,
renewable and recyclable products and made from wood grown in
sustainable forests. The logging and manufacturing processes conform
to the legal environmental regulations of the country of origin.

Printed and bound in Great Britain
by CPI Antony Rowe, Chippenham, Wiltshire

There's never been a day when there haven't been stories in **Amalie Berlin**'s head. When she was a child they were called daydreams, and she was supposed to stop having them and pay attention. Now when someone interrupts her daydreams to ask, 'What are you doing?' she delights in answering, 'I'm working!'

Amalie lives in Southern Ohio with her family and a passel of critters. When *not* working she reads, watches movies, geeks out over documentaries and randomly decides to learn antiquated skills. In case of zombie apocalypse she'll still have bread, lacy underthings, granulated sugar, and always something new to read.

Books by Amalie Berlin

Mills & Boon® Medical Romance™

Craving Her Rough Diamond Doc
Uncovering Her Secrets
Return of Dr Irresistible
Breaking Her No-Dating Rule

**Visit the author profile page at
millsandboon.co.uk for more titles**

Dedication

To my real Cousin Karen:

1. Sorry about the spelling change…

2. Thank you for all your support and enthusiasm for my books!

3. Childhood would not have been the same without you in it. Xoxo, Duh

Praise for Amalie Berlin

'A sexy, sensual, romantic, heartwarming and purely emotional, romantic, bliss-filled read. I very much look forward to this author's next book and being transported to a world of pure romance brilliance!'

—*GoodReads* on
Craving Her Rough Diamond Doc

CHAPTER ONE

THE SOUND OF screeching tires stabbed Dr. Kimberlyn Davis's ear. One by one every one of her major muscle groups seized, stopping her cold on the Manhattan sidewalk, tensed for impact. One burst of sound, then another and another—rubber on asphalt, metal on metal—her every heartbeat shuddering in time with each bone-rattling sound.

Teeth gritted, she twisted toward the street in time to see a body arcing through the air, arms and legs flailing for purchase in the already warm morning sun. A man. A motorcyclist. He tumbled, rolled and came down chest first on the grille's edge of a still-moving black SUV. The second impact tossed him back—a human pinball thrown and battered far more than flesh and bones could stand.

Her clamped jaw held back sounds she couldn't control enough to stop, a whimper that burned like a roar—searing her throat and blazing a trail down her chest to the still-bothersome scar that would forever mar her cleavage.

She should've run when she'd heard the first sound of squealing tires. Away from the danger. But she had taken an oath.

Before the cascade of car horns died off, before the vehicle he'd flown into had even managed to stop moving, Kimberlyn forced herself to start. One stiff step, then another, each step loosening her muscles and allowing the next to come easier, faster. Off the curb. Onto the street. Within three paces she was running.

Moving cleared her mind. One act of willful defiance in the face of her fear, her memories, let the next one came easier.

"Someone call 911!" she shouted over her shoulder.

Please, don't be dead.

She kept her gaze before her long enough to plot a course, then through the windows of every car she passed en route to the man.

She's okay.

They're okay.

Awake with head laceration.

Okay.

Okay.

Of course this was how her first week in New York should start.

By the time she reached the motorcyclist he was wholly beneath the SUV and several feet from where he'd landed. Dragged by the front bumper. The driver looked stunned through the shattered glass. He had a gash on his chin and another smaller cut above his left eye, but he was awake, moving...

Over the past year she'd gone from running from accidents to running toward them—but it always felt wrong. Even the times she'd come on the scene after the carnage had been wrought, her very soul had vibrated with the wrongness of it.

Wrongful death. All her fault.

From the first wreck she'd passed on the highway after her accident—when she'd been three months post-op, still in a cast, and on the way to yet another session with her physical therapist—she'd forced her mother to stop the car so she could get out and help. And she hadn't stopped since that accident. Couldn't stop.

Only the top of her current patient's helmet showed his

location under the SUV and the only thing she could feel at all good about was the lack of engine noises. It must have shut off during impact.

"Check breathing," she whispered to herself, words slipping in a steady stream through her lips as she talked herself through the things she needed to do. Order of operations. Mental checklist for emergency scenarios. Only action could keep her focused, let her ignore the tangle of emotion rotting in her gut.

It was also the only way to try to block out Janie's face, always with her—cut, battered and swollen—at the back of her mind. It became harder to ignore in situations like this.

"Bashing damage to chest. Get to his chest..."

If his heart still beat, he had a chance. If she got to him fast enough... Nothing could guarantee survival. Even if he appeared stable, some injuries just took longer to kill you than others.

"If the patient can't come to you, you go to the patient. Gotta get under the car..."

She dropped her backpack as she fell to her knees and scrambled over broken glass. Craning her neck, she looked under the car to see if anything besides the helmet had been snagged.

She couldn't see much besides that he wasn't moving. To try to take control of her mouth, she began to narrate on purpose—the habit drilled into her as an intern so that the patient knew what you were doing. And on the off chance that he could hear her...

"Sir?" Sir, because this patient wasn't Janie. Sir. A man. A man she didn't know. Not her fault. Not her fault, not this time. "Keep still, I'm going to come under there with you."

Her voice sounded shrill even to her own ears. Anyone would know she teetered on the edge of panic, but she wouldn't fall headlong into it. She had control. Always. Always. But if her patient could hear her, she should be comforting him. Making him confident she'd help him, not squeaking like a cartoon mouse. Her throat refused to loosen, but she forced a few more words through. "I'm a doctor... We're going to get you out of there."

Her heart banged a couple times, popping out of rhythm as it tended to do when dosed with adrenaline. It would settle down. It was nothing, a flutter. Pay no attention...

"Not answering...not moving..." The whispering started again, and something new—the slow, hard beats of her heart, an insistent reminder of the emotion she tried so desperately to ignore. He was never coming out of this. There was nothing she could do.

Be optimistic...

Straightening, she looked around the street to the closest group of people, eyes skating from figure to figure. No police to help yet...

Get under the car. Take a light.

Ripping open her backpack, she fumbled inside for the kit, glad for once that she had to keep it with her.

Once the dented silver case was in her hand, she flipped it open and snatched out the penlight. With only her light clutched in her hand, she looked around again for help.

Running toward her through the scene she saw a figure in ceil blue, the color of the scrubs she also wore.

Someone with appropriate skills coming to help...

She flattened to her belly and crawled under the SUV with her patient. When she was beneath far enough to reach his wrist, she felt for a pulse. Present...but weak. She continued to narrate, as she'd been taught to do. The practice was supposed to help patients manage their own fear in emergency situations, but it saved her from drowning every time. Even now, when the man didn't move or answer her.

She ran her light up and down the motorcyclist's body, looking for points of contact with the vehicle. Nothing. No snags. No parts of his body pinned beneath wheels. It didn't look as if he had any points of contact with the underside or the vehicle, except for where the bumper had snagged his helmet.

"Is he trapped?" a man's voice yelled from beside her, his words only just registering above the noise of the street and the roar in her ears.

Kimberlyn backed up carefully, doing her best not to bloody herself on the broken glass. When she finally got out, she took the light out of her mouth and straightened to look at her helper. The embroidery on the left breast of his scrubs showed the name of her hospital, where she'd been headed for her first day.

The name DellaToro stood out on the tag beneath the logo for West Manhattan Saints.

Him. Enzo, her cousin Caren had called him. At least she knew he was knowledgeable and skilled. He'd help her.

From the narrowing of his gaze as it rolled over her own embroidered name, he recognized who she was, too.

Neither Caren nor her new friend Tessa had told her how good-looking the man was. Dark hair and olive-skinned, deliciously scruffy. Shockingly dark blue eyes beneath eyebrows built for brooding... No wonder he was so used to people doing what he told them to. Difficult to argue with a jaw that square—made him look hard and unyielding. Like granite. Sexy, sexy granite.

Perfect time to think about the man's attractiveness. *Goodness, what was wrong with her?*

The answer hit like a slap in the face. His face had blocked out Janie's. That was why she'd noticed, and why her cheeks tingled.

What she needed was for her patient's face to replace Janie's. He deserved all her attention. But DellaToro's scruffy good looks would serve as a guilt shield until she could get that helmet off.

"The helmet is wedged under the bumper." Breathlessness replaced her shrill tone. Was that better? "But it doesn't look like there's any crushed areas or snags. We have to get him out from under there."

"But the helmet is wedged?" He bent to look, then felt around to where it was caught, apparently coming to the same conclusion she had: there was no foolproof way to get him out from under there. "We need to be careful of his spine."

"I know, but a perfect spine never did anything for a dead man. I can't even tell how he's breathing like this. Or if his eyes are open." Or show her inner demon that the motorcyclist wasn't Janie, even though she logically knew that couldn't be the case. "We might be looking at head trauma, too. We have to push the car off him." She turned toward the sidewalk and the closest pedestrians and called, "Guys, we need some help pushing the car."

DellaToro straightened to look at the group she'd called to. The group that wasn't moving at all to help them. He then knocked on the hood and yelled to the driver, who had found cloth in his vehicle to put pressure on his bloody wounds. "Put it in Neutral."

The man nodded, still mentally with it despite the blood on his face. Should she check on him? He could die from lack of attention while they worked on one man whose chances were much slimmer, by appearances.

She had to stop finding points of comparison. This wasn't her wreck. That man wasn't Janie, either.

Then, in a far more commanding voice, Enzo faced the rubbernecking pedestrians and pointed to two specific men. "You and you, help us roll the car."

The authoritarian edge to his voice seemed to work. The men who had ignored her just moments before came down onto the street, shedding jackets and dropping whatever they carried to come to the front hood.

Figures. Also not worthy of examination right now.

Ignore the handsome doctor's jaw, help the patient.

His attention turned to her and he continued giving

orders. "Reach under and get your hands around the edge of the helmet. We'll push it. You hold his head in place as well as you can."

Kimberlyn maneuvered herself to the man's head. With her cheek mashed against the front bumper, she strained under the car to get her hands around the edge of the helmet. "Got it." A pause. "Don't let it rock."

If it rolled forward even an inch, it might also snap both their necks.

"We won't."

At least Dr. Granite Jaw had a plan for this. All she had was grime from the street, a lurking wave of panic and glass shards sticking to her scrubs.

With the three of them pushing the SUV, they managed to roll it smoothly back. Pressure was released from the helmet. She eased her hands loose and when his head held position she flipped the visor open.

Finally. Another face to quiet guilty echoes in her mind.

Young. Very young. Closed eyes. Fast breathing. Still no response.

Had that been how she'd looked? Blood loss sped up respiration and heart rate as tissues and organs became deprived of oxygen, so it stood to reason that it was. Except she'd been pinned inside a vehicle, and the blood loss had been mostly visible, not hidden inside the chest cavity.

As the SUV continued to roll, revealing the man's body, she reached for her bag again and her kit.

DellaToro joined her, unzipping the man's protective leather jacket. At least he'd had the protection of sturdy clothing.

"His breathing is labored," DellaToro announced.

Of course it was. She'd take comfort in him still breathing if she didn't know how quickly that could change, and give them all a really bad day. One heartbeat to the next, things could turn, and the person you thought was most stable...

Focus.

"I've got some…"

She stretched to where she'd dropped her backpack and then tore into it. "Here, Dr. DellaToro." She produced a stethoscope and handed it to him.

"Thank you, Kimberlyn. Heard you were coming." He used her first name while taking the instrument.

Was that some kind of dominance display?

Not the time. Correct later.

She dug into the engraved silver kit again. The fact that she could act now steadied her. Those images of her wreck were still there, always there, even a thousand miles away—but now they lurked on the periphery. The rabbit hole she never wanted time to go down.

Just a little longer.

She extracted the gauze scissors and began cutting down the front of her patient's T-shirt, exposing an already forming bruise. Deep purple stippling slashed across pale flesh, right over the sternum. Bad bruise forming. No way would it be unbroken, and a broken sternum didn't protect what was inside very well. Bruising organs at least. Heart. Lungs, maybe. Bashing damage could be more destructive than bullets.

She bent forward to listen to her patient's breathing as Enzo listened to his heart.

Enzo. She could do it, too.

"Steady, but fast and faint…" he announced, pulling the stethoscope from his ears to hang from his neck, and bending to grab for the penlight she'd been using under the car.

"Faint?" She repeated the word—as if she didn't already expect that exactly to be the case. As if it could be anything else.

Her fingers searched his wrist, and she could barely feel anything but her own thundering pulse. "You're sure it's beating?" She fumbled beneath the edge of the helmet to find the carotid, looking for a stronger throb. Her fingers tracked over corded vessels. The jugulars stood out as if he was straining.

Distended veins in the neck. Symptom number two that she'd both expected and dreaded.

The carotid didn't stand out at all and she felt nothing pulsing in the general region. Blood backing up in the veins and not pumping through the arteries—reason for the distended veins.

"Pupils responsive," Enzo announced, then listened again. "Faint, but still fast. Maybe speeding up."

She should be doing that, announcing her findings as she went. Just one more second, one more symptom... Make sure...

He hadn't picked up on the diagnosis yet. She'd share as soon as she confirmed the third. Even if she was already certain what her fingers and eyes told her, she needed something solid to reference.

Her hand shot into her backpack again, but books and sundries blocked her search. She upended it and dumped the contents onto the pavement. The wrist BP cuff she still carried with her rolled free—her second guilty security blanket. She grabbed it and wrapped it around the man's wrist.

"You carry a cuff?" Enzo asked, but he was listening to her as he went back to the abdomen and began prodding gently, looking for injury.

Kimberlyn didn't answer, just pressed the button to start the automated machine and leaned forward to listen to his breathing again. "We need an ambulance. Did anyone call an ambulance?"

A beep announced the measuring of vitals had finished and she looked at the small display.

Pulse one twenty-nine. Pressure ninety-five over seventy-five.

"Crap. Crap, crap..."

Enzo's eyes snapped to her and then to the display on the little cuff. "That's not good."

"No," she said, looking around again. "Did anyone call 911?" Repeated it louder.

No one answered. The ones who'd helped push the car had already abandoned them. Enzo fished his phone from his pocket and dialed.

"We need a large syringe, and I don't have one of those in my bag."

Either he wasn't worried by the situation or he didn't realize the extent of what was going on.

"Enzo, listen to me." She used his first name this time to capture his attention. When his eyes met hers, she had to force the words through her clenched throat. "Cardiac tamponade."

Attention captured. "How do you know?"

"See the veins in his neck? Fluid's coming on fast, filling his chest, and there's no time for the pericardium to stretch and accommodate it to let his heart beat right. Either blood or serum. Probably both. Preferably more serum than blood." More blood would probably mean a tear, but serum could just be trauma.

A cold pit opened in Enzo's middle. They were close to the hospital, but that was the kind of diagnosis you wanted to say *after* remedying it.

He barked their location into the phone and followed it with, "Possible cardiac tamponade." After demanding two additional crews and the NYPD, he ended the call and stashed his phone again. The borrowed stethoscope replaced the phone at his ear and he listened hard. The faintness bothered him. "You think pericardial effusion from the impact?"

She nodded, and from the lack of color in her face he believed her. No one could go pale for show like that.

He hadn't had a cardiac tamponade patient in his four

years of residency, but she sounded certain and had the look of someone with first-hand knowledge.

Something had to be blocking the sound of the heart. If anything, the man was underweight, nothing else made sense besides a wall of fluid muffling the sounds.

Sam Napier, his best friend in the residency program, had warned him that one of the many women in Sam's House of Gorgeous Roommates had a cousin transferring in to chase Enzo's fellowship. He'd expected…well, someone sunnier in disposition and appearance. A duplicate of Caren's golden-blond curls, dimpled cheeks and the too-cheerful smiles that made it hard for him to be around her before at least two cups of coffee. Not this soft-spoken, dark-haired creature with the delicate features and soulful brown eyes.

"He was hit chest first," she said, taking the blood pressure again. "As in he landed with his chest on the front top edge of the grille of the car. Then bounced off. I've seen this before in another crash. Three big symptoms, Beck's Triad. Muffled and faint heartbeat. Distended neck veins. A narrow difference in the blood pressure readings… One, two, three." She pointed as she counted, chest, neck and the cuff. "There's barely anything between the systolic and diastolic."

The cuff beeped again, the new results darkening the screen. Pulse one sixty-two. Pressure eighty over sixty-five.

Damn. She really was right. He was either bleeding out or something else was filling his chest.

The sound of sirens close by caught his attention. They were only a couple of blocks from the hospital, and the sound came from the right direction. Closer than Dispatch, and coming toward them now. Lucky.

They'd have a defibrillator, and other tools…

He could hear her little cuff running again, beneath the blessedly loud siren of the ambulance as it rolled to a stop just ahead in the intersection. "You." He jabbed a finger at a woman in a power suit who still stood nearby, watching, "Meet the ambulance. Tell them we need a huge syringe." He placed the stethoscope on the patient's chest again, doing what little he could do to monitor the situation as help arrived.

Before the suited woman even got to the ambulance, the medics came running with a bag of tools, defibrillator and a large hypodermic syringe they slapped into his hand. His order had done the trick.

"Have you aspirated a pericardium before?" Enzo asked, looking at Kimberlyn. He hadn't. Normally he'd like to try, but she'd made the diagnosis. Even if it weren't a professional courtesy, he wanted to see her perform so he could gauge her skill level. It was the best way to ascertain if she was simply another trauma resident or an actual threat to his fellowship.

Whether she had ever done it before or not, the small brunette crammed her hands into the gloves presented by the medic and indicated an area on the right side of the man's chest, "I can do it. Swab around and between the fourth and fifth ribs." She joined him on the patient's right side.

He ripped into the alcohol prep and broke the canister within the squeegee to disinfect the area.

"Tell me if his heart starts sounding louder or if there's any other change."

Would chest compressions even work if the pericardium was full of fluid? It'd be like trying to squeeze a water balloon inside a larger, overfilled balloon…

Even with the stethoscope buds in his ears, he could hear the tremor in her voice. Still scared. Was she steady enough to perform the aspiration?

"I will." He listened and directed the EMT, never taking his eyes off Kimberlyn, "Get him wired up and on the monitor."

Cardioversion was possible now at least.

With the extra-large hypodermic in hand, she braced one elbow on her knee for support and explained. "I'm going from the right side because the heart juts to the left, and I don't want to hit it."

Yeah. Don't hit the heart...

She looked steady enough now. Whatever had her fighting panic, it came and went in waves.

Enzo backed up enough to make room but stayed close enough to keep the stethoscope in place to listen while the monitor was hooked up.

This might have been a bad call. She seemed competent except for those nerves. Her nerves triggered his. If she ended up doing more damage... Maybe they should just move him now and hope he lasted another five minutes, or however long it took to get to the hospital.

With her arms steadied and braced, she waited patiently the long seconds it took for the electrodes and wires to be placed.

He listened hard, holding his breath to cut out as much sound as possible. His own pulse sounded in his ears louder than what he was hoping to listen for...

Closing his eyes helped, cutting down the external stimuli. Without vision in the way, he could hear the heartbeat faintly in the background. Fast. Very fast. And with an abnormal rhythm.

This heart didn't just inch toward failure, it galloped. The man would never make it to WMS.

What kind of fibrillation—atrial? Ventricular? He opened his eyes and craned his neck to see the green line denoting the rhythm tracing across the black screen of the monitor.

The line swung wildly in an undulating wave that told him nothing.

Check the leads.

Okay, check the placement of the electrodes.

He grabbed an extra electrode and placed it beside the

one that looked somewhat off-center, then reattached the lead. The line settled into the regular, horizontal position, allowing him to really see the points.

Ventricular fibrillation. And tachycardia. He listened again, with his eyes following the line. The sounds were almost too faint for him to hear—something that backed up her diagnosis: there had to be a massive amount of fluid compressing the heart. "He's in V-tach."

"Thought he might be. His time is running out." She breathed in. When all hands were still, she breathed out slowly as she pushed the needle into the man's chest.

She could've done this a thousand times. Smooth and slow enough to be cautious but quick enough to feel the texture of the different tissues she penetrated. Her eyes had taken on that out-of-focus quality that came with pinning all your attention on feeling your way to a site unseen. He'd seen that look on the real pros so many times—an amazing ability to visualize the path through and the imagination to picture the diagnosed problem. It almost felt like sorcery.

As she drew back the plunger, bright, arterial crimson began to fill the clear tube. As pressure was siphoned off, the heartbeats became a little louder, a little more distinct.

She withdrew the full syringe and looked at him, those eyes dark with fear...not the exhilaration he'd expected. But, then, he'd never been in this situation, either. Exhilaration was hard to come by. Something entirely more primitive took its place.

"No change?" So hopeful.

"Still in V-tach." Enzo listened a few more seconds to give him time to convert. He tried counting beats but found it impossible and shook his head. "No change." He gave the heart a few more seconds, listening again, then shook his head, "Clearer, but still distant-sounding and out of rhythm. Drawing off the fluid wasn't enough to convert him to normal sinus."

She paused another few seconds, pinned by those soulful

eyes. Dr. Ootaka, his mentor, counseled distance. Emotions clouded reactions. Enzo had never had reason to doubt this mantra, though right now he couldn't claim to have that distance. He wanted to give the hope her eyes begged him for.

Hoping wouldn't get the job done. "I've never dealt with this. How did they do it at your old hospital?"

"The only one I saw treated was done in the hospital and they used imaging equipment to verify the diagnosis and location of the fluid before they aspirated." She answered quickly, her focus returning, and her voice firmed as she spoke. One word led to the next, and she focused on the EMT. "I need another hypo. Bring two, just in case."

She'd only seen it done once. Ugh. At least she didn't look it. Move past it. Enzo gestured to the defibrillator and she followed his gaze.

"Not yet. He's already banged up enough. Let's give him one more chance to convert. Honestly, it's not electrical, it's the pressure in his chest. I doubt cardioversion would do any good for him unless his heart stops entirely."

She rose on her knees and shouted toward the back of the medic, "Bring epi if you have it! Enzo, start the cuff again. I want the pressure before and after each draw." With a fresh alcohol prep she swabbed the area where she'd just gone in, readying the chest for another puncture.

Long, torturous seconds passed and the other medic arrived. As soon as the pressure was displayed, she pushed through with the second needle.

Enzo watched another rush of bright red fill the tube. It looked thinner and more translucent than it had before. "It's part serum, or he's filling with more serum than blood now."

"Good. The pressure might stop his heart still, but maybe it's not an aortic dissection. Buys us some time."

If it was only a small cut in the aorta rather than a hole through it, they had a chance of getting him stabilized and to the hospital before he crashed.

He concentrated on what he was hearing—the monitor couldn't tell him how loud the heartbeats sounded so the stethoscope was still needed. It was easier to look at the monitor—or even the dark, eggplant-like bruise on the man's chest—than at her worried face. He could tell from her complexion that she was normally a warm tan, but today she looked pale and fragile. Not a great look for a trauma surgeon. Even a trauma resident.

With the second round of pressure relief, the speed of the man's heart slowly decreased and the rhythm began to convert to something closer to normal. First, a few normal beats amid the pre-ventricular contractions. Then louder. Then steadier.

"It's working." He pressed the button on the cuff again and then leaned back to place the stethoscope in her ears, holding the chest piece over the heart again. He let her listen as she was the one performing the procedure.

After a few seconds she nodded. "I don't want to go again, I might hit the heart. The less fluid that's in there, the closer the pericardium is to the heart, the less balloonish padding to protect it." And they didn't have the luxury of imaging equipment here to see how thick that fluid balloon was.

"Agreed." Enzo checked the cuff again. "One hundred and forty-three over eighty-one." The tension that had held him stiff and hard in the preceding moments left in one rushing wave, so swift his shoulders slouched forward briefly.

Without thinking, his nearest hand landed on the back of her neck to lightly squeeze as he directed her gaze to the cuff. Her skin felt hot beneath the ponytail she wore, and his palm prickled where it touched her.

"Blood circulating again," she whispered, her breathless smile hitting him square in the chest. Shared relief. Before he could think it through, he pulled her into his arms for a hug. She sagged against him, her hands fisting in the back of his scrubs.

Apples. Her hair smelled faintly of apples, and something earthier. Clean. Sweet.

The comfort was fleeting as within seconds she'd stiffened. Her hands released the material of his shirt, reminding him it wasn't the time to be hugging this stranger with the soft womanly curves, or smelling her fruity hair.

He let go and put a little distance between them. What was worse, looking overly familiar or overly emotional?

Color had returned to her face and was focused on her cheeks now. He'd definitely crossed some line.

Right. "Get a line in him, and we'll ride with you." He redirected his thoughts to the paramedics, who really didn't need to be told what to do except that they'd come to a scene with two surgeons running things.

Kimberlyn left the cuff in place but went about gathering the contents of her bag as if the contact had never happened. He reached for his cell again.

Ootaka answered on the first ring. "Dr. Ootaka, there was an accident a few blocks from the hospital. Assisting with a cardiac tamponade. Thought you might want a heads-up to meet the ambulance."

The conversation was brief. A neck brace and helmet removal later, they lifted the man onto a backboard, then the stretcher, and trotted for the ambulance.

"He's on call today?" She climbed into the ambulance after the stretcher had been rolled in.

Enzo nodded, keeping his hands off her even though his natural instinct was to help her into the ambulance. "He's going to meet us." He stashed his phone and jerked his head in the direction of the hospital. "I'm running. Keep our patient alive. It's only a little way to the hospital."

Some physical exertion would help. So would avoiding any enclosed spaces with her. Good for all concerned. Or good for him, which was the important bit. And she wouldn't have to worry that he was about to hug her again. What the devil had that been about? He was happy about the patient, but still—weird.

Probably some kind of natural instinct in the wake of all that fear and hope warring on her face roused his protective instincts. Unfortunately.

He closed the doors, banged once to let them know it was safe to drive and then took off at a run for a nearby alley. Three blocks by vehicle, one on foot.

After her showing up on the scene, even if Ootaka would've been put off by the emotion, he still would've been impressed by the woman's knowledge. Which was okay, so long as Ootaka remained most impressed with him. Enzo hadn't fought his way through school and years of residency to lose it at the eleventh hour to a little scared Southern nobody...

If his luck held, Ootaka would meet him at the ambulance bay and he'd have a couple of minutes to speak with him before the ambulance—and his shiny new competition—caught up.

CHAPTER TWO

E<small>NZO MET</small> D<small>R.</small> T<small>AKEO</small> O<small>OTAKA</small> at the ambulance bay doors. Normally, sprinting a block would do very little to his heart rate. Not today. Today he was winded by the time he jogged through the automatic doors. Winded and annoyed. Off his game.

The older Japanese surgeon stood waiting, leaving Enzo no time to work out his problem. He barely had time for a good breath. Ootaka stared past Enzo to the empty ambulance bay, a look that demanded answers.

During the past four years, and especially the past year when he'd largely been Ootaka's primary assistant, he'd become used to anticipating Ootaka's questions from his expression alone. So he answered, "I ran ahead. It was faster on foot and I wanted a better chance to brief you."

And it's hot, he wanted to say. Hot and muggy, which no doubt contributed to his elevated pulse and respirations.

He took another deep, cleansing breath and launched in, giving the pertinent details even as he heard the sirens drawing closer to the building. "Massive bruising, likely fractured sternum, probably some ribs, too, but structure mostly intact."

From where the ambulance bay was located, he could see the vehicle turning into the parking lot. If he wanted to ask, it was now or never.

"I expect that there will be a need for surgery." He

waited only long enough for the usually taciturn surgeon to nod, and added, "I'd really like to stay with the patient and assist you."

Underhanded? No. Smart.

She'd been the one ahead of the curve with the diagnosis and field aspirations. While he wouldn't ever claim the spot of underdog, or let himself be relegated there, winners made their own fate. Preemptive maneuvers. Offense, not simply defense.

Besides, Davis had to learn sometime that the laid-back Southern lifestyle wouldn't fly in the city—something she clearly needed to work on, in addition to learning some leadership qualities. Let that be her second New York lesson: if you want something, you have to fight for it. Everyone wanted something, so chances were if you wanted something, then someone else wanted to take it away from you.

And that was enough justifying. What in the world was wrong with him?

He blew out a steady breath as his vitals came back under control.

"Let's see what we have, then." Ootaka finally spoke as the ambulance rolled to a stop, triggering the automatic doors. They moved off to one side to clear the route for the stretcher.

Ootaka stood with his hands at his sides, placid and waiting attentively. No indication anything was amiss.

Never in his entire career so far had Enzo ever felt this rattled in front of his mentor.

Only one person in the hospital had ever been able to rattle him, and they had an unspoken agreement of avoidance.

Even while watching his fellow residents fall out of the grizzled surgeon's favor, Enzo had always been the one in control and confident in his abilities. He knew Ootaka's rules. He understood the detached perfectionism that made up nearly the entirety of his operating-room demeanor. His professionalism, steadfast confidence and resolve were perfection in Enzo's eyes. Ootaka was precisely the kind of surgeon Enzo wanted to be. The best. Second to none after Ootaka retired. There could be no better place to learn that than Ootaka's OR.

Tension rolled over his shoulders and down his arms. Not like Ootaka's relaxed stance. In the reflection of the glass doors he could see his own arms...hanging at his sides, but stiff, ready for a fight. He rolled his hands at the wrist and settled. Shaking his arms out would only look even more affected.

He couldn't avoid Davis as he did Lyons. Did he even want to? He took an inventory of his goals. Staying on top would mean a better understanding of whether she truly was a threat or just another future ex-contender. Having a good understanding of his obstacles was the only way to overcome them. It was the not knowing that had him rattled. Once he had figured out the situation, there wouldn't be any weird emotional responses to taint Ootaka's opinion of him.

Whatever it took. Even if it meant angering a new colleague when she figured out he'd outmaneuvered her. But what did that matter to him? Another fact for her to get used to. She would've had to anticipate the sharp learning curve to come into the program this late in the game, and there was zero chance of her assisting on her first day anyway.

Ootaka never trusted one of his patients to anyone with untested skills. In that light, his request wasn't anything more than a formality when you got down to it. Asking first just showed initiative, a good practice. He wouldn't feel guilty about it.

Bonus: it'd give Ootaka an easy out if Davis came in asking, because she'd definitely want to assist. Helpful, like someone he'd want around for the next two years. As she exited the ambulance, Enzo added, "There was another resident on the scene. The transfer, Davis. She rode in the back with the patient."

"I wondered why she wasn't here yet."

In addition to untested surgeons in his OR, Ootaka also hated tardiness. The man kept an updated list of sins that could get you banned from his OR forever. She probably hadn't a clue about them. His action now might actually save her career—give her time to learn the rules before she went in blind and violated them. It was a good-guy thing to do. The idea that her competence might come into question because she'd been late saving a life didn't sit well. He could throw her a bone, let Ootaka know she'd made the call and aspirations.

"She—"

As the first word came out the two EMTs, Davis and the gurney rolled in, the little motor on the wrist cuff whirring to take another reading.

Ootaka cut in, "Who diagnosed the cardiac tamponade?"

"I diagnosed Mr. Elliot's tamponade, Dr. Ootaka." She immediately answered the question while still passing through the sliding doors.

All the mousiness he'd glimpsed earlier was gone. That was something at least. She recognized Ootaka on sight, which really shouldn't surprise him—she'd transferred in for his fellowship if the rumor mill was to be believed. She'd have done some research.

Though Ootaka was hard to miss. He had a kind of forbidding quality to his expression, even when he was in a good mood. Smiles actually involving his mouth were rare. Ninety percent of his expressions were in the eyes.

"The aspirations are what stabilized Mr. Elliot." He rolled with the name they must've discovered on the way. "Brought him back into normal sinus rhythm. He was in V-tach before the serosanguineous fluid was drawn off."

She still wouldn't be asked to assist, but she deserved to observe. It'd be the honorable thing to do, help her get a

foot into Ootaka's OR in a way she probably couldn't un-
wittingly screw up.

At the scene he'd noted at least three behaviors Ootaka
would cut her over: inability to speak with authority; lack-
luster leadership skills; and visible displays of emotion.
From the sidelines she'd be able to get a feel for things
without being in the spotlight.

"It had stabilized him, but he's popping more PVCs than
he was, and his blood pressure range is narrowing again,"
she added, directing all attention to the patient and the display on his wrist. "One hundred over seventy-five."

Enzo had gotten used to being the main one to answer
questions or brief Ootaka on patients. It was only to make
sure that he knew the whole situation that Enzo tacked on,
"Pressure had normalized to one hundred and forty-three
over eighty-five after the second aspiration."

"One hundred and forty-three over eighty-one," Davis
corrected.

Right. No more giving her credit. Those four measly
points didn't make any difference to the situation, other
than highlighting that he'd made a tiny mistake. Not precisely underhanded but kind of snotty all the same. Apparently she was capable of a modicum of backbone. But
squabbling over insignificant details wouldn't impress Ootaka, so he held his tongue.

Ootaka nodded in the direction of Trauma 1 and led the
way. In less than a minute the stretcher was locked into position amid the equipment in the trauma suite, all gloved
hands on deck.

"Davis," Ootaka directed. "Another aspiration."

Davis? *Damn.*

A larger hypo than the ones she'd used on scene landed
in her hand. A nurse took over the job that Enzo had per-
formed earlier, swabbing the chest.

Again he watched Davis carefully position and guide
the needle into the man's chest, then another flow of bright

blood pulled back into the hypodermic. Not so watery as it had been on the second draw.

"For the third draw, it's a lot thicker than it was even the first time."

Enzo locked his jaw to keep quiet. Something he never did with the other residents...but this was Davis's show.

Davis withdrew the needle and concluded, "His chest isn't simply filling with serum again. There's bleeding. He's got a tear somewhere."

"He does," Ootaka confirmed. "Going to have to go in. Correct call, DellaToro."

Of course it was. Enzo stepped forward again. Before Enzo could do more than nod, Ootaka turned to Davis. "Welcome to West Manhattan Saints, Dr. Davis. An OR has been prepped. You're with me."

Enzo's head jerked back as if he'd been slapped.

Ootaka had invited her to surgery.

A slower step back to get out of the way again and Enzo found himself blinking, as if clearing his vision would do something to clear up what he'd just heard. But nothing had changed. The situation settled like lead in his belly.

Ootaka was definitely impressed with her.

The man told all the first-year residents they couldn't assist him until he'd seen them in the OR to weigh their ability. They observed, he gave them small tasks, and gradually built up to assisting. Usually other surgeons did much of the initial surgical instruction, Ootaka was next-level surgery. And if you didn't meet his expectations...

It wasn't so much that Ootaka made a production of letting the resident know they were no longer welcome—big displays of emotion were the same as big displays of drama—he simply stopped extending invitations. It usually took the resident a few weeks to realize they were no longer welcome or even on his radar. Enzo had even seen the man forget the name of residents once he'd stopped shining attention on them.

Davis wasn't precisely a first year, but it was her first year at WMS. Ootaka had never seen her perform.

A pericardial aspiration by hypodermic, while tricky, didn't compare to using a scalpel...

The team wheeled Mr. Elliot out of Trauma 1 and down the fastest hall to the OR, leaving Enzo to find something else to do.

A now-familiar Scottish brogue came from just outside the door. "Kimberlyn got Ootaka already? Caren said she was good." He looked around the door frame.

"Don't make me hit you, Sam." Enzo stepped out, uncrossing his arms to let them hang, feigning the relaxed appearance he'd rather others see. He just couldn't get his shoulders to loosen up. "What are you doing down here anyway? Aren't you supposed to be with the babies?"

"I came to make sure Kimberlyn had made it, actually. We were going to walk together today, but I ended up needing to leave early for an errand."

"Miss Scarlet needs an escort?"

Sam gave a low chuckle. "She really did get under your skin."

"She's not under my skin. It was a quick reference to that dark-haired Southern pretty girl thing she's got going on." Enzo had lied, and he wasn't a liar. It was a point of pride that he could be blunt and honest about anything. She'd thrown him off his game for a third time. "It takes more than a strong base of medical knowledge to impress Ootaka. She's got steady hands, but her leadership is nonexistent. Couldn't even rally some rubberneckers at the accident to call 911 or to push the vehicle off the patient."

"Want to grab a pint after your shift? You can find some pretty lass to take your mind off Cricket."

"Yes," Enzo answered, because a beer sounded good, as did the idea of finding a *pretty lass*. Someone more his flavor. Not dark and soulful. Davis probably wrote poetry and wore black all the time when she wasn't in scrubs. Also not a lass. That sounded entirely too much as if it could fit Davis, and he'd rather have someone real. Overly emotional just didn't do it for him, either.

Hold on. "Did you call her Cricket?"

"It's her nickname. Don't tell her I told you."

Enzo snorted, but nodded to his friend—Dr. Cricket's new housemate—and headed off to look at the surgery board. Maybe they'd be in one of the surgeries with an observation gallery so he could at least watch...

A short walk and he stood, looking the whiteboard over. Head of surgical residents Dr. Gareth Langley had taken one of the rooms with a gallery. The name Lyons stood out on the list. He looked only long enough to determine he wouldn't accidentally walk in on that man's surgery, then moved on. Ootaka had indeed reserved the last gallery.

If he hurried, he might even avoid accidentally running into Lyons on the way. That had been the other bit of information to stand out on the board: times and approximate duration. His father was the last person he wanted to see today. Or any day. The fact that they frequently shared a hospital made it impossible to avoid him altogether, but Enzo did his best. Always did, and he imagined Lyons did, as well. In four years they'd managed to avoid saying even a single word to one another and that level of avoidance couldn't happen without two people actively working at it.

He relaxed only when he'd stepped through the door leading up to Ootaka's gallery.

In his time in the program nearly all of his competition had fallen by the wayside. Winning this fellowship was a marathon, but Davis was here to sprint the last leg. An immediate invitation into Ootaka's OR definitely meant she had started the sprint and he felt as if he was standing still, which was ridiculous. She couldn't cover that much distance in one surgery.

Time to get his head back in the game. Observe the new surgeon. See how much of what Sam had said was actually correct. See if she really was a threat to his goal or if his mind was playing tricks on him. However unlikely the possibility might be, he needed to judge for himself. If her backbone wasn't full-on displayed, it didn't matter how much she knew. She wouldn't threaten his position as favorite horse in the race for Ootaka's final fellowship.

But it might do the pit in his gut some good to see her getting the unavoidable dressing-down coming her way.

God, he sounded like a petulant child wanting Daddy's approval. His stomach churned.

No one could survive Ootaka's surgery without learning his particular rules. He should feel sorry for her.

If her arrival hadn't felt like another shadow he'd have to fight his way out of, he might actually muster some sympathy.

The only way to find whatever was bleeding inside Mr. Elliot's chest was to crack it.

Kimberlyn had been in a few thoracic surgeries since the accident, during the last months of her first year back... but seeing a chest open still made her scar burn.

This was someone else's sternum, someone else's pain.

The words danced through her mind on repeat every time she started to feel her chest tighten or her heart speed up.

Mr. Elliot deserved undivided attention, and the likelihood he'd one day have his own scar to fixate on hinged on the talent and skill of his surgical team. Mainly Ootaka, but she mattered.

Luckily, Ootaka was the best. One day she'd be that good—another mini-Ootaka to save those poor wretches who had to be cut out of ugly car crashes. Just as she had.

Ootaka's fellowship was the reason she'd come north. He announced last year that it was the last fellowship he was going to do, which was why she had ended up transferring to West Manhattan Saints when she'd been set up perfectly and had enjoyed her former hospital.

Waiting two years to apply for his next fellowship? No longer an option.

The intention toward trauma hadn't really existed before her accident. She'd thought about it but had floated between cardiac, cardiothoracic and plain old general surgery, too.

Her life had become a series of dominoes that day...

As much as she hated what had happened to Mr. Elliot, his pain was her good fortune. It had gotten her noticed immediately. Now she just needed to perform well in this surgery. Keep Ootaka's attention. Build his appreciation and belief in her. Do everything in her power to make this year count. Keep her promise: save the good people like Janie from the bad people like *her*.

Or, better, save the victims so the idiots who'd caused the wreck could learn and avoid turning into her. Normal lives for all involved. Two birds, one stone. That was a worthy goal. That would make her worthy.

Which meant outshining Ootaka's star pupil, Dr. I'm-Running-Ahead...

"Suction."

So Ootaka started her with the basics. Minding the blood was important enough. Suctioning it off where he needed to see what he was doing, keeping an eye on the pressure to alert him when they needed to give fluids...

Which was now.

"He's lost a...bit of blood," she began. Assisting a surgeon for the first time always meant getting used to the way they liked to do things. Very few things were standard when it came to OR etiquette. Hence her needing to ask, "At what point do you like to hang blood?"

"Are you saying that you believe we should be doing so now, Dr. Davis?" Ootaka never took his eyes off the patient, but movement in the corner of her eye pulled her gaze up. Someone in the gallery.

Enzo. Could he hear them up there?

Okay, she was being paranoid. Why would that matter? If he could hear, maybe he'd just pick up on how to be professional and not sneaky with a colleague.

Focus on the OR, not on who lurked above it.

"Yes, Dr. Ootaka. I would like to give him some packed red now."

"Better. In my operating room, do not couch your concern for the patient in question. You're a surgeon. Asking questions you know the answer to makes you sound uneducated. Save your questions for when you really don't know the answer."

Right. She could do that. Most of the surgeons she'd worked with preferred deference, but maybe that was their way of keeping a hierarchy in place. Ootaka's air and reputation did that well enough—maybe he had no need to force protocol through some etiquette dance.

"Yes, Doctor. I'll remember that." While she usually handled change well, not knowing how she was to behave wasn't one of those changes she could just float with. If she wasn't supposed to ask questions, did that mean she should just do what she thought was best? Mr. Elliot was Ootaka's patient now, not hers.

He did glance up long enough to look her in the eye. "Yes?"

"Does that mean for me to go ahead with what I think is the right decision, or—"

"No. Announce first with clear intentions and reasons. Always reasons." He'd started to sound a little annoyed, so she was happy when he immediately switched back to the subject. "Why packed red cells?"

As far as reprimands went, it wasn't much of one, but all corrections made her cheeks burn. Luckily, the surgical mask kept anyone from noticing, even if the inside of her mask was getting a bit stuffy.

Before moving to carry out the task of replenishing the

man's blood, she answered Ootaka. Minimize chance of rejection or reaction. Saline could do the job of plasma for now. Oxygen depletion to traumatized tissue was best avoided, so red cells were her choice. Reasons anyone in medical school would know, let alone a fifth-year surgical resident.

But at least there was some comfort in the sameness—questions and answers accompanied all lessons, no matter what hospital or surgeon you were with. She looked up at the galley again, and this time Enzo was looking at her. Not just watching the table. When she looked up, his gaze was locked on hers. Her belly trembled.

How was she supposed to keep her eyes on the patient with him staring? Correction: staring and smirking? Or was that a grimace?

Ignore him.

With the Q&A finished, she ordered the packed cells and another bag of saline.

So he could hear them. Whatever. Not that she expected any less from her competition. Caren had warned her he could be a jerk. He'd wanted to assist. She'd seen it in his eyes when Ootaka had invited her into his OR. And what was that about him being right about the need for surgery? She had to wonder what else he'd told Ootaka after running to get there first. She should've run with him. Only that would've meant leaving Mr. Elliot—and even for a couple of minutes she couldn't have made herself do so, knowing that neither of them would be with him.

What she needed to do was not think about him as an attractive man. Focus on the jerk, not the jaw. The arrogance. And all that jaw did was frame a smirking mouth.

Jerky, not to mention manipulative. *Keep our patient alive* indeed. Those words had assured she'd stay put.

But, worse, they'd made her feel important enough that she'd hardly questioned why he wasn't riding with them in the ambulance.

They'd made her underestimate him…

Later she'd send Caren a crankygram—an email she'd no doubt check in a couple of weeks. Maybe she could find Tessa after the surgery ended to get information. See if her new friend knew Enzo's tactics. Plot some ways to outmaneuver him, or at least figure out his usual manner of manipulation. It would certainly behoove her to know what his weaknesses were. Aside from arrogance.

Or maybe just vent. His attempt to maneuver the situation hadn't worked out so well for him this time. Maybe she didn't need to try to learn to do that. Maybe it was just a case of where the cream rose, and she just needed to focus on herself and…stuff. That's what she'd like. Avoid confrontation. Be pleasant and easy to work with. Be the person that everyone liked, or at least felt no overt hostility toward.

Be exactly who she'd been before the accident. That'd be awesome.

And impossible.

Think later. Pretend Caren had been overreacting when she'd focused on how hard Kimberlyn would have to fight for the fellowship.

CHAPTER THREE

SIX HOURS OF surgery later, Kimberlyn edged onto a stool that one of the post-op nurses had been kind enough to place beside Mr. Elliot's gurney.

This wasn't her usual routine. She usually avoided Post-op due to the confined quarters, activity and motility required for the staff to attend all the patients. Although her feet and back ached from the long day, and although she could swear the screws she would always carry in her femur buzzed and itched from standing in one position for hours, the manner of their meeting made it impossible for her to leave his side yet.

Distance was already an issue with this patient. Something she should work on.

Within the past year there hadn't been many patients who'd delivered gut punches like this, but she could still recite the names of each one, along with the big facts. How they'd presented. How they'd been injured. Procedures required to save them. Major complications. Length of hospital stay…

And she could recite even tiny details from the chart of the patient who hadn't made it.

"So, you were at Vanderbilt before transferring here?"

There was so much activity in the ward she hadn't even noticed him entering. The surgery had become like that at around the two-hour mark, when Ootaka had given her bigger tasks. They'd taken up more space in her brain, letting her stop worrying whether she was going to make some etiquette mistake or what Enzo thought about her performance.

Part of her wanted to know why Enzo had come to Post-op now, the other part just wanted to sit and rest. And stop thinking. Stop comparing. Stop bracing for impact...

Sometimes people pulled through open-heart surgery only to die in Recovery or the surgical ICU—the reason she sat there. The first few days were the most tenuous. But here he was distracting her—her new and annoyingly attractive nemesis. Or possible nemesis. Working that out right now required too much brainpower.

"Yes." There. She'd answered. Maybe he'd go away if she wasn't chatty.

Obviously he could find out information about her from other places, much as she'd done before arriving. He'd known who she was on first meeting, after all. And now he was spouting questions about procedure at her alma mater. He knew she had her sights set on Ootaka's fellowship. The grapevine didn't just extend from Caren and Tessa to her. It went the other way, too. Enzo had a grape on the vine.

And he could just go squeeze that grape for juice.

He rounded the gurney to stand on the other side of Mr. Elliot, giving the monitors a look, though he continued speaking quietly to her. "And you're Caren's friend."

"Cousin," she corrected. Correcting him was surprisingly satisfying. No doubt a holdover from the irritation she'd been nursing about his *run ahead* and *smirky looming* stuff.

He turned his eyes to her. "Did she give up her spot in the program specifically to free up space for you?"

"Of course she didn't." The hotly whispered denial sprang from Kimberlyn's lips so fast she hadn't even really considered whether he was correct before speaking.

Had Caren done that? It was like her cousin to do something altruistic and then lie about it to salve people's pride, but... "She said she wanted the opportunity to go into the field with that professor and his mission to Cameroon."

A nurse approached to get vitals—as she must every fifteen minutes—and Kimberlyn became all too aware of how crowded Mr. Elliot's bedside had become. Her being there had been fine, but two surgeons bickering definitely wasn't fine.

With energy granted by indignation, she stood, pushed the stool back out of the way and headed out of the ward. If he was going to grill her, he could do it somewhere else. The patient needed rest, and the nurses didn't need the distractions in the already tight quarters.

He followed her out.

Once the door swung shut and they were alone in the hallway, she turned to face him.

"Why did you ask me that? It's a...really...rude thing to say. Insinuating that I'm taking advantage of her good nature and maybe wrecking her career or something." Confrontation. Yay. Was it too much to ask that they maintain a civilized competitive atmosphere based entirely on merits and...positive junk?

"I just want to figure you out."

He didn't look bothered to be called on his machinations. He looked relaxed, no longer smirking, and also as if his question wasn't rude or anything to get worked up over. He didn't even stand at attention now, leaning with one of those broad shoulders propped against the wall, arms crossed and weight shifted to one foot. A lazy angle made from his...admittedly nice...athletic lines and other angles.

Not what she was supposed to be focusing on. Kimberlyn forced her gaze back to his.

"And I want to believe that you are a decent guy despite having been told otherwise, but the only reason I can think of for you to ask me that is because you want to put me on the defensive. Make me uncomfortable in my new program."

Mission accomplished. That, along with the sudden re-alization that she was doing exactly what strange men did to her: ogling his body. But that was her making *herself* uncomfortable.

When her eyes locked with his again, his brows lifted a little. Busted. But at least he didn't comment on it.

"I'm curious about you. Most people don't change pro-grams in the final year. It's too hard to rebuild your sup-port system and reputation in a new hospital. Makes this seem like some kind of impulse decision. A short-term goal. Not a career choice."

"Choosing trauma as my specialty, or choosing this fel-lowship as the one I wanted?"

He nodded. "Both. You just decided a couple months ago, right?"

"No. I decided before I began my fourth year in resi-dency." When she was in the hospital for other reasons besides work. The very thing she'd spent the whole day trying not to think about, and which she had no intention of revealing to him. Her stomach crunched and growled in a way that was part hunger, part nausea. Perfect. "But I really don't owe you any explanations about my or Caren's motivations. I'm here. I'm not leaving. You can't intimidate me or scare me into changing course."

"I'm not trying to do either, Davis."

"You're just trying to figure me out," she repeated, dis-belief making her fling her hand through the air. "Fine. Here's all you need to know about me—I'm good at what I do. In fact, I'm so good at what I do I'm not going to play games with you. I'm not going to scheme or run ahead to try to get to Ootaka first to get what I want. That's not who I am, and it's not who I want to be. You want to help me figure you out? Because right now, after having had a day to think about it, I'm having a hard time being charitable in my assessment of your character. You were great on the scene. Actually, I was extremely thankful that you were there. But then you spent the day smirking at me from the gallery. And now this?"

Once she'd started, it got easier to say what she thought about his behavior, too easy. She'd feel guilty, but her words looked to bother him about as much as a sunny spring day bothered daisies. She knew that people were blunter up north, but dang...

Before she lost her gumption, she whispered hotly, "And just for the record, I know what DellaToro means. From the bull, or of the bull...and obviously it's missing a final word." The half-whispered words could've passed for a two-year-old with her first introduction to whispering.

He smiled at the end of her tirade, uncrossing his arms as he chuckled, which was at least better than all the smirking. "Feel better?"

"No!" A bit mean and snotty, actually. And immature, and ridiculous that she'd taken the long way around saying the *S*-word... Lame.

"Did you see that condition a lot at Vandy?" He asked again.

Back to digging for information...

"No." Again she denied first and then had to pause and consider. He'd managed to rile her up, but that didn't mean she had to stay riled. She could chill out. If she let that little fire he'd built in her gut go out, he might not see how emotionally battered the whole day had left her. Depriving him of information had started to seem like a valid survival tactic.

To give her mouth a chance to chill, she took her time leaning against the wall facing him, across the several foot divide framing the doorway bay into the SICU. "I saw it once at Vandy. But I have the symptoms etched on my brain. It was in the back of my mind before I even reached him. I expected it the second I saw him coming down chest first. You shouldn't feel bad about not knowing at the time. It's really easy to miss."

There. That was more like her. Nice. Helpful. That's the kind of person she wanted to be.

Enzo watched Davis's expression go from angry to gentle in the space of a few statements. Too smooth and practiced to be real. "So I'm rude, and I'm guessing *jerk* also wouldn't be far off your definition, but you're still trying to make me feel better about my mistakes?"

She smiled at him, a real smile with just a hint of something bratty twinkling in her eyes. And it was adorable. "Just because you're a jerk doesn't mean I have to be one, too. Besides, you didn't make a mistake. You just didn't know the answer. There's a difference."

No difference. If she hadn't been there, he would've made a mistake. That single thought had weighed on him throughout the long day. He had to do better than that. He had to be better than that. The only thing worse than standing in Lyons's shadow was the idea of never exceeding it.

On a personal level, Enzo already knew he was a better man than his father—he took care of his family and had started trying to do that at four years old and hadn't actually learned how to do it until his mother had remarried— but he had to be better than Lyons professionally, too. That was what the world judged a man by: his prestige. That's why Lyons was known the world over, but the world had barely blinked a year ago when his stepfather had died.

It wasn't so much he wanted Davis to make mistakes, but before today he'd always been the one with the answers. If he hadn't known something, none of the other surgical residents had known it, either. And maybe none of the thoracic residents, or cardiac residents.

A successful trauma surgeon had to know a great deal about a number of specialties to handle whatever might come up in surgery. Like today. Cardiac tamponade... He wasn't sure that a cardiac resident in his final year would've even gotten that—but she had and it had impressed Ootaka. And him.

"You're sweet. You shouldn't give everyone the benefit of the doubt. Sweet doesn't survive long here. New York chews up sweet people and spits them out." The words—the very idea—left a sour taste in his mouth. Right now, he was the main predator circling her because he had to have that fellowship.

He didn't want to be the one to chew her up and spit her out.

It was in that second that he realized he was attracted to her. When she'd been pale beneath her tan at the scene, he'd still noticed she was pretty but not in a way he'd had time to think about.

During the hours watching her in the surgery, he'd had few physical details to form opinions on—most of her had been covered in the protective gown, mask and cap. He'd been able to see she had a fluidity of movement that spoke of control and precision…grace. And she had the mental endurance required to focus on a task for hours.

Seeing her now, when she was tired enough that her defenses were down and she was no longer concealed by OR green, he could appreciate the delicate quality of her features and the hints at the shape hidden by baggy scrubs.

"Is that a warning of your stance on this fellowship?"

No.

"Yes," he said.

Ootaka's fellowship was the best anywhere. He wasn't just a trauma specialist; he'd completed separate fellowships in several subspecialties. Spending a couple years as his single student was like a crash course in Everything That Can Go Wrong in the Human Body and How to Fix it.

"So you sought me out to warn me about yourself? Or was that part of your study methodology to learn more about the condition and Beck's Triad?" Okay. Now she wasn't buying that she should see him as a threat, even though he'd admitted it. Either she was as confident in her abilities as he was, or she was playing with him. "I'm still kinda surprised you haven't seen the condition in the past year."

Earlier, at the accident and throughout the surgery, her accent had been suppressed. Now, tired after a long day, the more she talked the more he expected her to hand him a lemonade and invite him to the front porch swing.

Which was also adorable. He had to stop thinking those kinds of things... She was the enemy. In theory.

"It has happened in the ER here in the past year, but never when I was on duty. I'm sure no part of the city is cardiac tamponade deficient, but I haven't actually treated that condition before today," he assured her, and then backed up, something she'd said earlier refusing to stop echoing in his mind. "Symptoms etched in your brain from a condition you've only seen once? Makes it seem like you have some personal connection to the condition. Is that why you were expecting it?"

Her smile disappeared and she leaned off the wall, eyes leaving him to track to the door again. She didn't want to answer that question. It had roused the wariness his warning had failed to do. Good.

"I read and study a lot to keep sharp."

Lying. They were both lying, but he was just better at it.

"So all symptoms of emergency scenarios are etched on your brain?"

She plucked up the badge that had been left for her during surgery and got ready to buzz herself back into Post-op. "That's my goal."

Not lying.

"And I'm sure that they'll be etched on your brain from here on out," she added.

Still uncomfortable. Uncomfortable enough to flee.

"How long are you staying?" He nodded to the ward door, allowing the subject change.

She hesitated, fishing a watch from her pocket and putting it on. "I don't know. I might not go home... There's an on-call room, right?"

He nodded then extracted his card from the thigh pocket of his scrubs. "My cell's on the back. If Elliot takes a turn while you're here, would you text me?"

The way her brows lifted said that he'd surprised her. She hadn't expected him to care that much about the patient. Maybe his warning had done a small amount of good. With her hand outstretched, she stepped forward to take the card. "You're worried about him?"

Her words confirmed it.

"I do that on occasion."

Before he put the card in her hand Enzo took the little outstretched palm in his own. Small. Delicate like her features. Nice skin, soft, but she was obviously tired. "Your hands are cold."

Resisting the urge to rub some warmth back into them, Enzo placed the card on the upturned palm and curled her fingers over it. "If you're going to go home, get someone to walk with you. Our part of Brooklyn isn't bad, but it's safer in pairs or groups. At least until you get some city smarts, Country Mouse."

She couldn't slaughter Sam for that nickname.

A ghost of her earlier smile returned.

He let go of her hand and let her buzz herself back into the ward before heading the other way.

"Hey, before you go..." she said, from behind him.

He turned to look back at her.

"Really, thank you. For charging into the fray to help me and Mr. Elliot. Not everyone is willing to do that, put themselves out there when it's dangerous—physically dangerous—and also because of the litigation-happy society we live in. If it had been just me on the scene, Mr. Elliot would've died under that SUV. Doesn't matter who got to assist Ootaka. You saved a life today, Enzo."

Still being kind.

If Country Mouse wanted the position, she'd have to fight for it. She might yet figure it out. This was only her first day.

Kimberlyn adjusted the hang of the shopping bag on her arm as she walked beside Sam, one of the two remaining roommates at the brownstone that Caren, Tessa, Sam and Holly had shared—and Holly owned.

Holly was loaded and well connected, and both those things encouraged Kimberlyn to keep her distance for now. She already had enough stress to deal with.

Tessa had recently moved out of the house and in with her boyfriend, Dr. Clay Matthews.

Caren had left for Cameroon, leaving Kimberlyn to sublet her unit.

She hadn't seen much of anyone but patients over her first week, so an outing with Sam was just what she needed, and the green market was the clincher on her decision to come out. Spending time with someone else who didn't sound as if they were native to the area—or in Sam's case sound as if he was from anywhere but Scotland—was the perfect way to try to let go of the week's stresses.

Organized tables and stalls stretched far out in front of them, each one lined with small baskets filled with produce and fruits to tempt. It looked fresh, but fresh off the truck rather than fresh off the vine. Appearances could be deceiving, and this country girl could spot a hothouse tomato at twenty paces.

"This is the most orderly vegetable market I've ever seen. Our farmers' market is usually staffed by old men with beer bellies and overalls. They look like they hand-picked every vegetable, and sometimes they smell like they did it that morning. Though it's better to go out back in Mamaw's—er, my grandmother's—garden."

Since relocating, she'd been making a concerted effort to try to ditch the twangiest part of her accent, but if she wasn't vigilant, it kept slipping through.

"That sounds entertaining at least."

Entertaining, like listening to Sam talk, spending time with others rather than in her own head...where all she could do was think about Mr. Elliot.

Despite his body stabilizing after they had operated and repaired his problems, he had yet to wake up. His body was on the road to recovery, but his EKG had stayed depressingly flat. Not the rocketing recovery she'd hoped for him.

If he didn't wake up soon or show signs of activity, his family might have to make some hard decisions. If she hadn't been on the scene, they wouldn't have that unpleasant possibility looming in the future, a possibility that felt more certain every day.

But maybe he'd still come out of it. Wake up. It could happen. He was still recovering from the anesthesia and the powerful pain medications that went with the kinds of surgeries he'd had. He might wake up. Though even if he did, chances were slim that he'd be the same.

Worrying about him wouldn't help him. Wouldn't help her. But this trip to the market would, as long as she found a suitable topic soon.

"Sometimes. There is one old farmer who goes to the market we frequented...and everything he said sounded like a Southern preacher. Booming and dramatic. Even just talking about vegetables, I always kind of wanted to add to the collection plate..."

Sam's expression said he didn't know what Southern preachers sounded like. Right. Their different geographical histories gave them a misleading feeling of sameness.

Trying to make a new friend, and this was the best she could do?

What else? Enzo and the fellowship were pretty much the fixation of her every waking hour, but she couldn't talk about that, either, with Sam. Enzo and Sam were friends, and since Sam was her roommate she wanted him to be her friend, too… There could be no drama. Only niceness. And the quiet, neurotic worry that came with having an overactive imagination—whose imaginings now centered on all the ways Enzo could screw her over while she listed about, not knowing how to compete.

Sam led them off down the first aisle of Brooklyn's green market, and she yawned for the third time in the few blocks they'd walked to get there.

"Not sleeping well, Country Girl?"

Country Girl. Country Mouse…she might as well be wearing bib overalls and chewing straw…

"Not so far. All the noise. I thought I liked noise to sleep by, but with all the horror stories I've heard from everyone back home about the dangers of New York City—don't go getting a big head when I tell you this, but the only way I've been able to trick myself into sleeping is by imagining that I am safer in the house because you live there. My inner feminist really hates that I feel that way."

Sam grinned down at her, and was she imagining things or was he standing just a little taller?

"Strut all you want, Braveheart. If someone breaks in, I'll remind you about the strutting when you fail to go rushing in to defend us, or at least scare away all the would-be robbers or probable serial killers in a manly fashion."

"You're entitled to your fantasies." He didn't comment on the likelihood, but got back to her problem. "Get earplugs, maybe a fan or some kind of ambient noisemaker. Before too long you'll be too tired to notice the noise anyway."

"I'm already tired enough that if I didn't have to eat, I'd be uneventfully thrashing around in bed right now. I'm sure that my poor diet isn't helping me sleep better. Everything

I've eaten since I got here has either come from a vending machine, a box, or was served with fries on the side. My body is screaming for something leafy and green. And fruit. And possibly some manner of stimulant-infused ice cream. Energy drink companies should make ice cream. Comfort food and caffeine to help get through the transition. They have everything else in New York..."

It was all different. Different and scary. According to the rumor mill, Enzo had run off two different contenders for Ootaka's fellowship in the past year.

Run them right out of the program, and they'd switched specialties. Two in one year. So obviously it wasn't just her who found him intimidating and a jerk. And annoyingly handsome, though that probably wasn't what had run off the other contenders.

In all the times that she'd spoken to Caren about her transfer into the program over the past year, she could have mentioned those specifics. Maybe her cousin hadn't wanted to scare her off. Or maybe she just hadn't thought Kimberlyn actually had a shot at it. There were other trauma residents in the program. She could blend in with them and still get a darned fine experience and go on to a great fellowship. It just wouldn't be Ootaka's.

"I'll never get used to the heat," Sam muttered.

Small talk. Small talk. More small talk... Because this was how people made friends. At least, when there was no shared misery to bond them together.

"We have hot and muggy most of the year. Only when we have it, there aren't these enormous buildings blocking the view of the horizon. I never have to go far to see whether black clouds are rolling in, so I can tell if there's a storm coming to cool things down. Or I can see trees, and they let me know."

"Trees tell you if it's going to rain?" A male voice came from behind her.

Speak of the devil.

She'd only spent any measurable time with Enzo for one danged day, and Kimberlyn could already recognize his voice. And it had nothing to do with how nice a voice it was…though it did have a kind of velvety rumble that made her ears tingle. It was more about being alert, and that voice came attached to someone she'd really like to stop sneaking up on her.

She'd seen Enzo here and there, but she'd mostly seen his name on the surgery board. Despite Ootaka giving her a shot with Mr. Elliot, she hadn't been in any other surgeries with him since. Enzo had. Maybe not a bad thing for her, but definitely not helpful, either.

"Hey, man. She's in tune with nature. Just because the only green you've seen is in Central Park, or that weird girl with the green hair you dated last year…" Sam turned but Kimberlyn kept her eyes on the tables of veggies and fruits. There was a basket of tomatoes that wanted inspection, and if she didn't engage, the market might remain a nice diversion.

It probably shouldn't bug her that he was there, or that Sam was friends with him. But all the time she'd spent fretting and worrying this week came surging back. She'd nursed it through hours of surgery, staying by Mr. Elliot in SICU until the wee hours, through the phone calls to Tessa, scheming and digging for info, and reading yet another stack of journals to try to know everything—right now!

"She was a freak, but she was fun," Enzo said. She could hear the smile in his voice. "So how do trees tell you about rain?"

She turned and immediately regretted it. Out of scrubs, wearing blue jeans and a black T-shirt, he had that simple, manly, doesn't-give-a-damn-about-fashion-and-still-looks-amazing thing working for him.

"If you know what to look for, there are lots of signs in nature to give information. Like moss growing on the north side of trees. That kind of thing," she explained without explaining and then stopped and turned back to the vegetables. The more she talked, the more ammunition he'd probably have. Who knew what he could use? Maybe someone better skilled at duplicity. Someone who wasn't her.

"You're still generalizing. Specifically, how do trees predict weather?" He sounded interested, though it could be a cover for trying to make her look dumb.

But Sam also seemed interested. Sam was a good guy. She'd heard enough from Tessa and Caren to know he wouldn't be trying to set her up. And just like that, the air shifted and her annoyance started to subside.

"When the barometer and the winds change just before a storm, the leaves of many deciduous trees—the trees that lose their leaves in autumn—like to turn over. You look at the tree canopy as a whole, and if there's lots of patches of light green amid the deep greens of the top side, that usually means rain," she explained. "It's not foolproof, sometimes they flip over when the winds are blowing from something other than the usual direction, but in the hours leading up to a good storm in the warm months, it happens a lot. More accurate than the weatherman during winter."

"Sounds like superstition or old wives' tales," Enzo announced.

"Our wives' tales are more colorful than that." Kimberlyn put down the basket of tomatoes she'd picked up. They were much too perfect. Perfection meant hothouse. "Like if you need rain, kill a garter snake and hang it in a tree. But I've never heard of anyone actually trying that one. You know, since the 1800s."

"Could be true, though. The leaves, not the snake," Sam argued, though in a noncommittal way, and then shifted the thrust of the conversation. "I thought you usually went to your mom's for dinner on Saturday."

"I do. I am. Just thought I'd grab some strawberries for my girl on the way. She loves them."

His girl. Good. Dr. Sexy McSneakyFeet had a girlfriend.

She could ignore his attractiveness now as a matter of sister solidarity. Not that it really mattered. Dating was off the table until she got through her fellowship and got a practice established. Her training and education had to take at least 95 percent of her waking hours. Even if that meant listening to lectures in the shower and reading while she ate.

"You know you're always welcome to join us. Mom makes way too much food." Enzo and Sam talked food, too, which set her stomach growling.

"You know I'll come. Your mum's a much better cook than any restaurant I can afford."

They both turned to look at her. Was that an invitation?

Kimberlyn smiled to cover the nervousness coiling within her and pretended it didn't sound as if her stomach had given up waiting for food and was fixing to just digest her instead.

"Hungry?" her sexy nemesis asked.

Wasn't there some old saying about eating with your enemy? Technically, observing Enzo in his natural habitat could be related to her training. Eating with him and his whole family and the strawberry-lover? Yeah, that sounded like a bad idea.

"Don't worry about me, Sam. I can find my way back. You two go on. Get your strawberries there before they go mushy in this heat."

"You don't want to come?" Enzo asked, stopping her from actually running away yet.

"I'm sure it's really great and I appreciate the offer, but—"

"You're afraid we're going to poison you?"

"No." It felt as if she answered all his questions with *no*. "Don't be ridiculous. If anyone poisons me, I'm sure that Caren will tell the police to come straight to your house. So it'd be silly for you to try." Picking at him, acknowledging the conflict that had been flying between them since day one, somehow made it more bearable. It was actually kind of fun in a completely messed-up way that felt like playing... Something she should not enjoy.

Seeing his girlfriend started to sound like a better idea. Maybe that would help diminish his attractiveness, and making friends with his girlfriend so that maybe he wouldn't be too scheming over the fellowship was pretty much the extent of her manipulative abilities right now.

Enzo grinned. "Most of my family are Sicilian. We're not big on subterfuge."

"So, I wouldn't get poisoned, I'd get..."

Sam dragged a finger across his throat in dramatic fashion, making her laugh. "No, seriously, you should come. Enzo's my friend. You're my roommate and my new friend. I know you're both going after the same fellowship, but I like both of you and I'd hate to be stuck in the middle. Come. Eat. Call a truce for the day. You were just complaining about eating food from a box..."

"Yes, I was."

"And your stomach was complaining about eating nothing," Enzo pointed out, triggering another protracted growl.

She looked at Enzo, giving him a few seconds to shut the idea down. When that didn't happen, she pointed to a flower vendor in the next row over. "Okay, but I'm bringing flowers at least. My grandma would skin me alive if I showed up empty-handed."

CHAPTER FOUR

"OH, HELL."

Sam's expletive cut through whatever he and Enzo had been speaking about, not three feet away from the white wrought-iron fence circling Enzo's mother's home.

Enzo and Kimberlyn stopped walking and looked at Sam.

"I forgot about something I needed to do today. I have to go to the hospital."

"You don't want to go after you eat?" Kimberlyn asked, her gaze shifting from Sam to Enzo. They hadn't known one another long, but surely he could recognize a pleading look when he saw one. No way did she want to go in there alone, but she'd been hungry before even leaving for the market, before the walk of several blocks to get here. If she didn't get food soon, she might knock down Enzo and steal his strawberries. Maybe they'd pair well with chrysanthemums and daisies.

"I really need to go now."

Enzo accepted this with a quick shrug, "I'm sure Mom will send food home with Kimberlyn for you."

But that left her alone to talk, say dumb things and give Enzo ammunition, completely upsetting her plan to sit silently, smile, eat and listen to other people talking.

It was easier to listen. Easier on her nerves, and also a good way to learn about these people who were now inside the small circle of her life in New York. As much as she appreciated being included, her generally introverted, social survival mechanism was to blend into the background. Not having to talk facilitated that.

Sam had other ideas. After quick goodbyes, Enzo turned to Kimberlyn, gesturing her to follow him. "Let's go on in. You can meet my girl." He led the way through the gate and around the back of the house.

Right. His girl. How would his girl feel about Enzo bringing home another girl to meet the family? This day just kept getting better.

The back door opened straight into the kitchen and a sea of people. Was it a family reunion weekend?

Kimberlyn smiled to swallow her panic and closed the door. She'd never seen so many people for any sort of dinner besides the reunions her mother's family held, picnicstyle, every other Mother's Day at a park in the Smokies.

Enzo wove through the people. Kimberlyn stayed at the door. She might be able to run still... Maybe everyone would just be so happy to see Enzo that they wouldn't notice her sneaking back out the door.

"Mom, everybody, this is Kimberlyn." Enzo spoke loudly enough to be heard over the crowd, and suddenly the sea parted and loads of people—many of whom had those pretty dark blue eyes—looked at her.

Right. Speak now.

"Hi." Kimberlyn waved the flowers, reminding herself that they were in her hands, and slowly inched through the rapidly closing wake Enzo had left. "I hope you don't mind the extra mouth, ma'am."

She stopped near the older woman and held out the flowers, smiling to cover the fear scratching at her insides.

"Not at all. Thank you, Kimberlyn," Enzo's mom said, graciously taking the flowers and handing them to one of the younger women in the crowded kitchen to put in water.

The house had obviously been remodeled since it had

been built, with an eye toward making the kitchen as big as possible. It took up almost the entire first floor, as far as she could see. In the places where walls had provided support there were now simple wooden pillars to keep the house structurally sound.

Relieved of her cargo, Kimberlyn edged toward a pillar—her gateway to somewhere with a little more elbow room.

Although Enzo had been living in his own place for years, his mother's house still felt like home. Smelled like home. Smelled like dinner, too, thank God.

"You should've brought Sam with you, too," his mother said.

Enzo kissed her cheek and once Sophia was finished with the flower vase, he took his berries to wash. "I tried. He got all the way here before remembering something he had to do. Kimberlyn is his roommate. Just transferred into the residency program and the trauma track. Sam would be happy if you sent him a plate home with Kimberlyn."

That said, he looked to see that Kimberlyn had scrammed to the far side of the dining-room table, where she could sit and not have anyone directly nearby—everyone was either in the kitchen or in the living room, with the dining half of the great room in between.

He didn't see who he wanted, though. Raising his voice, Enzo bellowed over the crowd, "Okay, where's my girl?"

From the sunken living room, he heard the call, "Jo-jo-jo-jo..."

"Joe?" The look on Kimberlyn's face went from confused to amused as his baby niece barreled in his direction, crawling fast enough to silence anyone who said she wasn't as strong as any other baby her age now.

With the largest, reddest berry in hand and paper towels, he met Maya halfway in the dining room. Once he'd swooped her up and given her a kiss, he headed for Kimberlyn and the table. "She can't say my name yet. Zs are hard." She was never going to learn to say it properly if he didn't correct her, and he didn't care at all.

With skinny little arms around his neck, Enzo bounced her to one of the dining tables and sat near Kimberlyn.

"She's beautiful. Is she yours?" Kimberlyn tilted her head to get a view of Maya over his shoulder, where she'd been squeezing his neck. "I thought you were referring to your girlfriend. You know, at the market."

He laid the towel and berry on the table so he could maneuver the little wriggler with both hands, letting Kimberlyn really see the niece who'd stolen his heart. "This is Maya, and she is my girlfriend, aren't you?"

"She's mine," Sophia said from the kitchen. "Enzo just likes to pretend he did the heavy lifting when she was born."

"She's beautiful," Kimberlyn called back to Sophia, then focused on the two of them again.

Enzo picked up the berry and held it up. Maya seized it with two grabby hands and set about gnawing at her favorite fruit.

"I delivered her," he explained to Kimberlyn, whose brows rose in unison.

"She's your...?" She pointed to Sophia.

"Sophia is my sister. Maya is my niece, and she is my special girl so I bring her strawberries to buy her affection."

Kimberlyn smiled at him, widely and without even a hint of the apprehension he'd seen on her face since he'd gone to Post-op to talk to her and made sure she knew he was a threat. Suddenly, he wanted to give her a strawberry, too.

But that would not happen. If she wanted one, she could get one herself. He shouldn't be happy that she once again looked at him as if he could be the good guy, or someone she could be friends with. He sure as hell shouldn't be sitting at his mother's dining table with her, showing off Maya…

"I think your cunning strawberry plan is working, Dr. DellaToro." She shook out the damp towel, folded it and placed it back on the table, where he could get to it and wipe the red juice off the baby before she became unalterably sticky.

The softness in her eyes when she looked at Maya made Enzo want to like her.

"You thought I must have come from a family of ogres, admit it."

She smiled again. "I suspected you were raised by wild dogs, but maybe that's just what you want your competition to see."

"You think you're my competition?"

"I know I am." Her smile took on a cheeky edge that demanded he grin back at her, especially as she turned in her chair so she could watch the baby gnaw the berry and ooze pink drool everywhere. "And you know it, too, or you wouldn't be…well, the way you are with me at the hospital."

"Maybe I like to put on a scarier mask than is real."

"Maybe. Or maybe this is a trick, too. You could have bought that insanely adorable baby, for all I know. She certainly seems to like you well enough to be a paid actor."

Maya picked that moment to offer Enzo a soggy bite of her strawberry.

He mimed eating it and made *nom-nom* noises that made the baby laugh, and probably lost him some of his power of intimidation with Kimberlyn. But when he looked at her he found a wistful image that bordered on adoring.

His mother approached the table, laughing in her usual manner, and saving him from saying the wrong thing and simultaneously redirecting them both to the baby while singing his praises in one fell swoop. The woman could multitask.

She always could, as far back as he could remember.

Though maybe it had started when Lyons had walked out on the four of them and she'd been forced to raise three kids and hold down two jobs... It had been years before she'd remarried and their family had grown again.

Kimberlyn said something that shot past him. The next thing he knew, she'd reached out to touch Maya's big dark curls. "I'm sure if you brought this one into the hospital, she'd be the best PR in the world."

"All the people in the hospital who matter know Maya already," Enzo tossed out there, but didn't get a chance to say more. A hand fell into his hair and what started as a loving pet to the back of his head became the kind of tug that only mothers could get away with.

"Does Lorenzo have a bad image at his hospital, Kimberlyn?"

"Oh, no, ma'am. He can be just a bit intimidating to his peers. Not me, of course." And if he'd had any kind of winning hand before, he'd shown his cards when he'd gotten Maya on his lap.

"But maybe people who haven't seen him with such a doll on his knee..." Kimberlyn said, her accent slipping in as she joked with his mother, or maybe flirted with him?

That could be a suitable swap for powers of intimidation.

"Honestly, he's thought of as the top resident in the trauma rotation. I'm currently waging a war with him, though it only started Monday. We have a truce for dinner, but I make no promises he won't pelt me with peas or lob a spoon of potatoes."

Kimberlyn turned her attention back to the baby and felt something soften in her. Did he know what it was like, seeing a stupidly handsome, brilliant, successful man holding a baby? Like a mule kick right to the ovaries. So unfair.

It made it completely impossible to view him in the same manner she had, even as late as coming through the back door of his mother's house.

He loved his family, and he was completely different around them.

He loved his niece, too. He'd be a wonderful father.

And she had been totally flirting with him a minute ago. *Shoot.*

All that aside, it still felt like a foreign country to her. She'd been around people with big hands-on families back home, but she didn't have that.

Enzo's mom said something and headed back to the kitchen, leaving her with Enzo, the most beautiful and adorable yet slobbery baby in recorded history and the distinct feeling that she'd just been set up.

"You're a very hands-on uncle."

A powerful urge welled up inside to smack him on the back of the head and take his baby away. She'd accuse him of faking all this, too, if Maya didn't clearly adore him.

"I'm not the one who's special here. Maya is our little miracle. She was very premature, which is why they know her well at the hospital."

Kimberlyn looked at the baby more closely. She was small, and she had a more slender build and face, but she seemed normal despite that. Bright-eyed and rosy-cheeked, even before the strawberry. "How old is she?"

"Just coming up on a year."

Okay, she was very small for her age. "How far along was she?"

"Twenty-six weeks and three days. It was a couple of weeks into the start of my fourth-year residency at Saints and in my free time I was doing a ride-along one night a week with the local squad to get field experience. A call came in for Mom's house. I knew it was something to do with Sophia...and my squad responded. The baby was already coming when we got here. I delivered Maya over there in the living room."

Twenty-six weeks wasn't the death sentence it had been a couple of decades ago, but outside a hospital setting?

"Pretty terrifying," Enzo confirmed, reading her expression right apparently. "If she'd been born in a hospital at that time, her odds would've been great, but…" His expression firmed, and she knew he'd been transported back to that time. He'd have been calculating the same odds she was now calculating. At that point in development every day mattered, every day added a handful of points to the chances of survival.

You never want someone in your family to have roughly equal odds for survival or death…and especially not a baby.

Her throat thickened. She knew how the story ended up—she could plainly see that it had been a happy ending—but the emotion in his voice kicked her in the heart. And she knew better than anyone that someone could look perfectly normal and healthy but have myriad health problems beneath the surface.

He never looked at her, his gaze absorbed by the tiny baby girl in his lap gnawing on a strawberry and leaking pink drool everywhere. "We got them to the closest hospital, and about a week later I managed to get them transferred to WMS. She was in the NICU for a long time."

Which was how he and Sam had become friends, she understood immediately. In that moment she knew with just as much certainty that she'd definitely been set up to come to this dinner without him.

"That's why your mom asked where he was, right? Sam's got a standing invite?" Maya drooled on Enzo's arm and Kimberlyn picked up the paper towel to swipe it up before they got stickier. "I think we've been set up, Enzo."

"Sam?"

She nodded. "He's your friend, he's my roommate and one of the handful of people I know here. He outright said that he didn't want to be in the middle of us earlier."

And she could appreciate his position. She didn't want him to have to choose sides, either. Her longest contact with anyone in the brownstone had been a simple phone relationship until she'd finally gotten to the city and met Tessa in person—but she wasn't in the house any longer. She could see that kind of friendship between Enzo and Sam being a strong one. She could also see someone like Sam being the loyal type...

Enzo could've had a hand in the manipulation—it was a great way to let her know how much the fellowship meant to him: his family was his motivation. But he'd be playing it up if that were the case, and he'd looked as surprised by Sam bowing out as she had felt.

"You've gone quiet," he said.

"Just thinking." Not worth talking about, because even if Sam hadn't orchestrated exactly this situation, she just couldn't look at Enzo as the shark in the goldfish tank anymore. He was more than she had been giving him credit for. He had depth, and if he used every weapon at his disposal, she couldn't really blame him.

Change the subject.

"And I was also thinking about whether or not I should ask any questions..."

"About Maya?"

"She looks very healthy."

"She is very healthy now. Her lungs were the biggest problem, lagged behind as is normal. But she has no heart or digestive issues so we were very lucky. She needed help breathing for the first few weeks and had to have her system nudged to start producing surfactant. But we were incredibly lucky." He kissed the top of his niece's dark, curly head, and she grinned then showed him that her berry was all gone, nothing left but the stumpy bit at the end that no one liked to eat.

"All gone," Enzo said, refocusing just like that. He captured her drooliest hand and held it out for Kimberlyn to clean off. "We'll have another one after dinner."

Dinner had better be worth all this. How in the world was she supposed to keep her guard up when he was sharing a well-gnawed strawberry with a miracle baby and involved in cleaning tiny sticky hands?

"You have a nice family. It's not even a holiday and
you're all getting together to eat. You said weekly dinner
when we were at the market, but I guess I didn't expect…
well…like, twenty people at a weekly dinner."

He finally looked up from the baby and shifted her so
that she leaned against his chest and he could turn his
chair to face Kimberlyn. "You're not close to your family?
I thought you and Caren were close. Of course, I thought
that family values and togetherness was big in the South.
Along with cotillions and hoedowns."

She snorted, "No way. Hoedowns are so overrated. To
Nashvillian's of culture, it's a hootenanny or nothing."
When she was rewarded with a chuckle, she answered a
little more seriously, "They also still have cotillions, but
they're like the fancy-dress equivalent of civil war reenactments. Cotillion clubs exist, but I never had any desire to join one. And I think your definition of close and
mine don't necessarily line up. My parents are pretty busy,
I guess. They do their own thing. I largely did my own
thing, too. We see each other on holidays. I call once or
twice a month." She paused and looked toward the living
room briefly before asking in a quieter tone. "Has your
dad passed?"

It wasn't a subject Enzo liked to talk about, though for different reasons than why he didn't want to talk about Lyons.
"Ernst died last year. About two months before Maya's
birth," he answered, realizing in that moment just how
near it was to the anniversary. Which would bring everyone down if he pointed it out. Maybe she wouldn't pick up
on that. It would definitely change the flavor of the afternoon for her. For all of them.

But he should probably say something about Lyons. She
obviously didn't know Lyons was his biological father yet,

but chances were good that she'd find out. Rumors circulated through the hospital like a soap opera, and even though they didn't share a name—or anything else—someone would tell her about him. "My father..." He hated explaining this to anyone. "Ernst was my dad. My father is still living, but we don't have contact with him."

"Oh."

No, it didn't fit with what she was now seeing of his family, and maybe that's why his father had bailed—he hadn't really liked the idea of a close-knit family. Or maybe he had been, and still was, just a selfish monster who didn't want to know anything about them and resented reminders that they shared his genes.

The first year after Lyons had left there had been gifts delivered for birthdays and Christmas, and thereafter just extra money in the child-support payments to account for gifts. He'd found out that Lyons had even stopped asking about them around that time, despite his mother always reassuring him that his father was going to come visit soon... he was just very busy...

"I'm sorry. I didn't mean to pry."

"It's not a big deal." He jerked his thoughts back to the present. Talking about Lyons always did this to him. "You'll probably meet him before long, though. He's got privileges at Saints." He bounced his knee a little, refocusing on Maya—she was a happy addition to his family, and Lyons was neither wanted nor needed. Time to shift the subject away from the bad parts of his family history back to Kimberlyn. "No siblings?"

"No siblings. But you're right, I was closer to Caren. I had family in the area, but they were mostly older. Caren was the only one my age who lived moderately close, and between visits we were like pen pals, then phone buddies. Probably unsurprising, since we're the same age."

"Same?"

"Yep, our birthdays are less than a month apart."

"She's a year ahead of you."

"Yes," she answered, her expression becoming more guarded. The same look he'd seen on her face outside Post-op. Hiding something. Cagey. A hint of fear in the midst of sadness. Definitely hiding something.

"She was a year ahead in school." Kimberlyn's words came slowly, as if they were carefully picked.

Something happened. "Did you get held back a year?"

"No!" The shrill pitch her voice took on gave her expression the kind of transparency that Enzo always avoided. He'd just upset her inner perfectionist by even asking that question. "I was valedictorian. I decided to take a year off...a couple years ago."

What kind of driven professional would take a year off in the middle of their residency? No kind. Not someone with a choice in the matter at least.

"You took a break in the middle of your surgical residency?"

Kimberlyn sat back in the chair, her mouth suddenly dry. How could she explain it safely?

When she'd come back to her residency program after the accident people had treated her differently. Not because they'd thought badly of her—although they probably should have done—but everyone had watched her as if she was going to fall apart, physically or emotionally. Even if she wasn't wary of Enzo knowing too much about her past, she wouldn't want everyone at WMS knowing her medical history. She'd worked hard to get back on her feet, and they were now firmly beneath her. It wasn't a weakness to exploit, or wouldn't be if no one knew about it.

But she had to tell him something. Truth was, she didn't want to be the sort of person who always suspected other people of malfeasance. The only thing that could make sense here would be the truth. Besides, what kind of hypocrite would a surgeon have to be to fault someone for taking time to recover from several big surgeries?

In front of her was a man with a baby on his knee, surrounded by family and a pervasive feeling of goodness—a still-scary *abundance* of people who loved him. She wanted to tell him. Ignore the shark-shaped shadow he cast behind him, which everyone had warned her about.

Which was the real him, the one she could be friends with or the one who would see her as chum in the water?

Ugh, subterfuge. She sucked at this. "You're probably getting strawberry drool on your shirt." Trying to change the subject might be cowardly but it was the only truly safe thing to say.

The squint of his eyes said he saw through her tactic, but he went with it for the moment. "Strawberry drool would be the best thing I've had on my shirt all week."

He smiled, his eyes connecting with hers, and she looked deep. Gorgeous eyes, really. Intense. Sexy. Deep oceanic blue with a thread of golden amber toward the pupils. That gold gave them warmth...and she wanted to be suckered in by it. Being so far from home, immersed in the new hospital and a completely alien culture, she'd felt adrift. But as she looked into those beautiful hazel blues...

A loud clatter from the kitchen broke into her thoughts—she really didn't need to be thinking about him in the vicinity of the word *beautiful*. One metal pan on the floor triggered another fall, and the noise scared Maya. The baby let out a howl that proved beyond any doubt that her lung function was excellent.

Kimberlyn took advantage of the commotion and stood, gesturing around the large, open room. "I need the ladies' room." Lies, half-truths, covers for her limping sanity... She just needed a few minutes of solitude to try to figure out the best course of action before he started demanding answers. And he needed to comfort that baby.

This scheming and manipulation business was going to be the death of her.

Enzo gave directions while standing and cradling the screaming baby against his shoulder.

She slipped past him and the family at various seating areas through the house into the cool half bath for guests. Small, but a sanctuary.

Enzo didn't seem to be in on the scheming but it would've been a dastardly brilliant way of putting her off her game. But if he knew what drove her it could only hurt *her* cause.

He'd managed to run off two residents, and no one could tell her exactly how that had happened. They couldn't even confirm for sure that it had happened, only that they'd been there, they'd been competition and then suddenly they had been somewhere else. Since then no one else had gotten that close. People didn't run off or switch focus without a reason, just as she would've never taken time off if she hadn't had to. No sane person intentionally sabotaged their schooling, especially after all the effort required to make it that far.

Despite that year of therapy and recovery from the accident, the extended routine to get back up to fighting trim after the accident, her endurance still wasn't where it had been. Some surgeries could last well over twelve hours, and if she were asked to perform one of those today, she might not be able to.

She didn't honestly know if she'd ever get to that level. Her heart was in good enough shape to be considered normal, but she still had brief spells where it would go out of rhythm for a couple of beats. Not enough to be diagnosed or on medication, but it served as a constant reminder of what she'd lost physically in the accident. If this race came down to one of stamina, he'd win for sure.

But she couldn't live with herself if she didn't try. It was the only thing that made it okay that she'd survived that day when her best friend hadn't. Not okay, it could never be okay, but it could be bearable. She could become some-one worth the sacrifice Janie had made for her.

When she came back out, people were gathering around the table, and the conversations continued as if she weren't there. Just the way she liked things. Eat. Blend into the background. Go home. Figure everything else out later.

Maybe call Tessa and harness some extra brainpower, since she obviously couldn't make up her mind about any-thing with regard to Enzo.

CHAPTER FIVE

THE FOOD WAS GREAT, the cheerful atmosphere even better, and by the time Kimberlyn said goodbye she had a basket with food for Sam and an escort home.

What she didn't have was an idea of how to respond to or even process the evening. With a handful of blocks to travel, she'd have walked it alone if Enzo hadn't insisted on driving her. A quick car ride later and he pulled up in front of the stately brownstone.

She turned to look at him. "I have to ask you something. Did you run off two other contenders for Ootaka's fellowship? Because there are so many rumors floating around, and I thought that they fit the man you are at the hospital, but you're completely different with your family."

"Aren't you different with your family?"

Kimberlyn shook her head. "I guess. I don't know." And then she squinted at him. "Was that part of your plan, to bring me to your family's house and make me watch you carry around an adorable baby to make my love petals go all dewy? Because that's a dirty trick."

"Love petals?" He laughed suddenly, shaking his head. "That phrase should be struck from your vocabulary, Mouse."

"You didn't answer the question, Rat." Hah, Rat. Not the world's best comeback, but she was new to this verbal sparring thing. "For the record, an attractive, successful man carrying around an adorable baby is like a sucker punch in the ovaries for almost any straight, single woman. Probably even those who don't want children. There's just something alluring about a big manly man and a tiny help-less baby…" She shook her head and then faced him. "It would be like me showing up at your door in crotchless panties…and then taking your picture!"

"Taking my picture?" Enzo watched her with barely contained amusement. Not exactly the emotion she'd been looking to rouse in him.

"You know, flashing you." She grumbled. "That's what my grandma called it…when a woman didn't sit in a lady-like manner while wearing a dress. Off the topic."

"And the topic is?"

Kimberlyn squinted at him. "That you with the baby was a dirty trick. And it's not going to make me go easy on you just because you're sexy."

"You were planning on going hard on me before?"

He baited her—repeatedly—and she kept falling for it. Time to put a lid on that. "I was planning on being my best, and that's still my plan. I can be really obnoxious about knowing everything and answering every question. I know this about myself and usually I try to dampen it a little so that other people have a chance, but I'm not doing that with Ootaka."

His amusement faded a little, but not enough to show he was taking her seriously. "Noted." He lifted one shoulder, the half shrug of an unconcerned man.

She stopped with a sigh.

Enzo watched her deflate, but his mind still stuck on the idea of her showing up anywhere in lingerie. "Just for the record, lingerie allegories are not going to help clear anything up. All they do is muddy the water."

"Fine. So does a handsome man cuddling a beautiful baby." She went back to that subject with a resolute nod. "So if that was a tactic, it was completely unfair."

If she wasn't attracted to him, it wouldn't have bothered her. Though, really, it didn't go the other way. The idea of a gorgeous woman in lingerie would have sent his mind off track. It didn't have to be particular to this woman. The urge to torment her, though…definitely particular to this woman. "Are you trying to tell me that my holding Maya made you attracted to me?"

"No!" she blurted out and then sighed hard enough to fog the windshield. "Kind of. Yes. Just put me out of my confused misery. Are you the man I saw today, or are you a shark swimming through chum-littered waters? Did you—"

"I didn't run them off," Enzo answered, though why he didn't know. He'd encouraged those rumors in the past. They did the work for him and kept people wary of him and more easily intimidated. But after spending an afternoon with her, the idea of her thinking badly of him…

"What happened, then?" She leaned forward, picked up Sam's basket and settled it on her lap. Readying to make her escape.

"People need someone to blame when they fail." He shrugged. "I let them blame me, but I wasn't any worse to them than I am to any other resident. I pride myself on knowing the answers and performing at my best, just like you do. When someone screws up, I make sure they know why they screwed up. Some people don't take correction well."

"Is that it?"

"I may not have been very nice when I corrected them, but I've got no more authority over any other resident than I do over you. I've never chewed anyone out publicly, but I have privately ripped into anyone who jeopardized one of my patients…" As he spoke he could see, even in the low evening light, the war on her features as she tried to decide what to think. "And I don't see anything wrong with that."

She was quiet a moment and then gestured in a half-hearted way designed to express disagreement, or maybe just frustration. "Presentation matters."

"Not more than the message."

The quiet resumed. "I guess not," she said eventually, then asked, "So, where does this leave us? I know you warned me off you, but..."

It was Enzo's turn to choose his words carefully. He could feel the weight of those soulful brown eyes on him. The day had changed things...but the realization hit him that so had his opinion. It had been a nice day, and he was going to have to ruin it. "I want to put this nicely because I do actually like you, and I respect your skill and knowledge..."

Kimberlyn nodded when he paused, giving another gesture for him to continue. "I hear a *but* coming."

Do it quickly. Be honest. If he lied about this, it might save her opinion of him, but it wouldn't save his opinion of himself. "But I don't see you as competition for the fellowship."

Kimberlyn let the words sit for a moment, her brows pinching as she worked over the words. "You mean at all? It's only been a week..."

"I'm sorry." Why was he apologizing for this? Because she'd been with his family, she'd been great with Maya... and he owed her courtesy if nothing else. "It was a week that started with a bang. I admit it, you had me on my toes from the moment we met. I was very concerned."

"But I did something wrong," she filled in, the slight wobble to her voice letting him know that she was working to keep her words and voice level.

"Not exactly..." Enzo grimaced. "You haven't made any mistakes that I know about. And I am sure that Ootaka is impressed with your ability to diagnose and perform the steps that kept Mr. Elliot alive, and you did a good job in surgery, outside that one thing."

"Get to the *but*."

"But…you're very gentle." Gentle. It felt like some kind of slam against women to use that word on her in that fashion, which he didn't like at all. He tried again. "Your natural inclination is to be sweet and deferential. Those aren't leadership qualities. When he takes on a fellow, Ootaka is looking to remake himself. He's looking for someone commanding and self-assured."

"It was my first day and the first surgery. Do you think I won't have any other opportunities to perform with him before the end of the year so I can tell if I'm…improving?"

She didn't take his choice of words like macho rubbish but, then again, someone sweet and deferential would give him the benefit of the doubt in that. An example of what he'd meant, which he'd feel like a jerk pointing out.

"I don't know if you'll have other surgeries with him or not. You might. You might not. If you do, keep in mind that he's not going to correct you on the same thing twice. And you're probably going to be left with as many questions about whether you are doing better in his eyes after future surgeries as you do right now."

"I see." Kimberlyn said the words as a kind of verbal pause. She didn't really see, but she'd never been somewhere that being deferential was a bad thing before. Her upbringing had drilled into her the importance of respect. She'd even given her stuffed animals the appropriate deferential titles. Her stuffed walrus was Mr. Waldo, not just Waldo.

Without deference as her go-to position, she wouldn't know how to behave at all. It was in her to always try to be kind first…but she'd never had a combative support team in an operating room. Outside a general sense of leading the team, she couldn't even picture a situation where she'd have to throw her weight around with her surgical team.

The scent of food that she'd found delicious only a couple of hours prior now smelled heavy and made her feel a touch queasy. Kimberlyn shifted the basket out of the way and opened the car door. "Thank you for telling me. Your advice. Dinner…" She was waffling. It sounded like a pathetic cut and run even to her own ears. "And the ride home! Don't want to forget that. I'll make sure that Sam drops the basket off at your mom's."

Kimberlyn closed the door before he could say anything else and headed for the brownstone's steps at a trot.

She hadn't reached the first step before hearing the other car door. She kept going. "What are you doing?"

"Walking you in." His voice sounded closer behind her.

"Unnecessary. I'm almost to the door already." The weight of the basket in her left hand lifted as he commandeered it.

He'd probably just call Sam to invite him inside if she said no. And he had invited her to dinner with his family… Swallowing a sigh, she unlocked the door and stepped inside. He followed.

The common areas of the house were extremely nice and tidy. The kind of elegant niceness that made Kimberlyn hesitate to put the food down anywhere but the kitchen. The food he was carrying anyway.

He followed to the kitchen.

"Obviously you can see that I'm inside. So what is it you really want?" She turned and propped her hip against the counter, arms crossing.

For the first time since she'd met him Enzo looked uncertain. Even when they'd met at the accident and he hadn't dealt with a cardiac tamponade before, he'd still never looked uncertain. He'd been unflappable. And now, of course, it didn't last, but it was there, a fleeting furrow of his brow that said words he'd probably never admit to.

"You're upset," he said.

"So? You aren't responsible for my happiness." For someone who avoided confrontation, she sure ended up arguing with Enzo a lot. "Don't expect me to cut tail and run to obstetrics because you don't think much of my chances with Ootaka. I'm here to try and I'm going to do that to the best of my abilities."

"Good. I want you to. But you have got to grow a thicker skin. Become a crocodile." He closed the distance between them and placed his hands on her shoulders, keeping her facing him and holding eye contact. "And just so you don't have any room to run this around in your mind later, I don't usually give pointers to the competition."

"Like you said, I'm not the competition," she muttered, realizing as the words came out how childish she sounded. She usually did so well with accepting criticism in order to improve. Her skin was usually thick, like a rhino's.

"Hush. I'm trying to say that I like you. Even when you're..." He stopped, his gaze going from her eyes to one of her shoulders, where his fingers were tracing over the thin cotton of her shirt and the still-thick and welt-like scar crossing her shoulder. "What's this?"

"It's...nothing. It's just..."

He pulled the neck of her shirt to one side, exposing the site of one of her incisions. "What was this?"

"A knife fight," she joked, because making up a story felt entirely more fun than talking about her actual trials, tribulations and the barbed-wire, booby-trapped obstacle course she'd run the past two years. "But it was one of those plastic knives you take on a picnic. So it took a lot of sawing back and forth to make a substantial enough cut to scar like that."

Before he held the shirt to the side to cause the neckline to bag and reveal the meatier, more worrisome scars, she pulled the fabric from his hand and covered herself again—neckline up to her eyebrows, just how she liked it. "Repair of a torn rotator cuff. And it's healed now. I had lots of therapy and it's fine. Didn't affect my dexterity at all."

She held the affected hand out for his inspection, steady as a rock. No shaking. Surgeon's hands, and an injury that had worried her sick for months wondering...

Shake it off. Prove to him that it was steady. She went through a series of arm motions to show the range, twisting her hand, forearm and full arm at the shoulder. No catch. No issues. Proof.

He lowered his hands, let his arms hang at his sides, then apparently thought better of it and crossed them. The muscles down his forearm corded, echoing the sudden tension in the room. "That's not why I asked."

If he didn't consider her competition, would it even matter if he knew a little bit about the accident? Outside him maybe treating her differently. He'd been the one to start the relationship off on the wrong foot. Not relationship. Well, professional relationship. Which was where she was going to file that thing he'd said a second before discovering the scar. He liked her. As a doctor and colleague. Not in a sexy way. And she didn't like him in a sexy way, either. And didn't even want to, no matter what her emotions had been saying at dinner.

If she just came clean—or cleanish—it would definitely save her from having to come up with some reason for the injury that he might not even deem acceptable anyway.

All the subterfuge, weighing words and jockeying for position, could make her give up before she even really got going with the year.

"Okay. The truth is that I've seen both sides of the trauma table. I was in an accident. There were some surgeries that patched me back up. I'm better now."

"That incision site is still pink. Not quite the angry red of an immediately recent scar but definitely not more than two years old. Is that why you had the break mid-residency?"

"Yes."

More truth.

"What other surgeries?"

"Does it matter? I'm fit now. If I don't have a completely clean bill of health, then it's just a little dingy. Like a coffee dribble on your scrubs in the morning."

She gestured to her chest, realized that she'd more or less pointed him at the evidence of having her chest cracked at around the same time, and quickly gestured at her thigh instead—where he'd find another scar if he looked. Darn it! If she didn't give herself away with words, it was with body language.

"You're the one hiding surgeries, so you tell me if it matters," Enzo muttered, taking a step back away from her to lean against the counter, rather how he'd leaned outside Post-op. His jaw bunched as he apparently gritted his teeth...out of sync with that lazy lean.

"It doesn't matter to the job," Kimberlyn said quickly, looking him in the eye steadily, willing her words into him. "Yes, I've had some obstacles to overcome on my way here, but we all have our obstacles."

He wasn't buying it. She could tell from the way those dark blue eyes became little more than squinty slits. "Why wouldn't you want anyone to know that?"

"Because there are always consequences to obstacles you have to work through. Funny me, I thought one of those consequences might be that you used it as a reason to limit me. And you know, you told me right out of the gate not to trust you, so why would I tell you any of this?" She grabbed Sam's food basket and went to shove it into the refrigerator. If nothing else, she could save him from some dreaded spoiled-food disease. "All that matters is I've recovered. And I don't want anyone thinking that I can't do something before even giving me a chance to do it."

"And you thought I was the bogeyman, that I'd use a torn rotator cuff against you."

Not even a question, he'd just made worrisomely accurate deductions about her motivation to keep things secret.

"Yes," she confirmed, for once starting a response to him with something other than the knee-jerk *no*. "Again, not entirely my fault. You warned me, and you *do* have that reputation for being lethal to the careers of competitors.

And before you even say it, I know you don't consider me competition right now, but that'll change. I didn't come all this way to fail."

He didn't need to know how far she'd actually traveled. Not just the hours and hundreds of miles she'd driven to get from east Tennessee to New York City, the metaphorical road had been even harder to travel.

When she turned to look back at him his features had relaxed again and now matched that lazy lean a little better. "Okay."

"Anyway, the consequences are personal. I grew up keeping personal stuff personal. I don't have that big beautiful family background where hugs abound, and everyone talks and laughs and catches up with each other on a weekly, if not daily, basis. I don't know how to be that... sharing. Especially with virtual strangers."

"Okay."

"Okay?"

They eyed one another warily.

Kimberlyn was the first to crack. "What does 'okay' mean?"

Enzo stepped closer and reached out to take one of her hands, forcing her to look him in the eye just by the way he focused on her. "I'm not going to use your trauma against you, okay? I'm going to help you."

"Why?" Her voice broke over the short word, the deep eye contact and warm hand holding hers overwhelming her senses. Her skin buzzed where they touched, and the physical sensation grounded her even as his gaze skewered her. It all added up to a connection that made it seem as if he truly did care. Lord, she wanted to believe it. And that was wrong, too.

"I like you." A rueful light shone in his eyes, making her believe him.

He did like her.

If a simple touch could make her insides tremble, how

would it feel to have his arms around her? To be skin to skin down the length of her body?

It couldn't happen but, oh, she wanted it to.

"So, I'm going to tell you something I've learned in the past four years. You know Ootaka's guidelines he keeps on the bulletin board in the locker room?"

He was still talking. And this was supposed to help her.

She nodded, trying to concentrate on what he said rather than the feel of his larger, warm hand in hers. How much bigger was it? How would his warm olive complexion look against the rosy tan she'd inherited from deep Cherokee roots? Her eyes tracked down to look and watched his square thumb stroke the back of her hand, firm but tender. A manner of touching she recognized, even if she hadn't felt it in a long while. He wasn't lying. It wasn't a trick. He liked her.

And was truly trying to help. "I know the list," she whispered, her voice refusing attempts at any volume. She had to stop this hand-holding thing. What was she, twelve?

"Memorize it."

"What?" Kimberlyn pulled her gaze back up to his as she extracted her hand. This touching and talking thing could not work. One or the other. And the talking she needed.

A crease appeared between Enzo's brows as she pulled her hand away, but he got on with what he was saying, clearly not as affected as she'd been. "Memorize Ootaka's guidelines. Really think about what each one means. It's the reason I said I didn't know if you would be invited back to his OR. He really is trying to remake himself every time he takes a fellow. And when the other surgical residents failed to live up to his expectations—the points on that list—he stopped inviting them to his OR. That's why there are so few people I consider competition. He's not going to choose someone who doesn't follow his guidelines."

Without the connection, her brain started working again,

clicking through what Enzo had said as it applied to her situation. She'd violated that list her first day in the OR. Before she'd had a chance to read it.

It put him running ahead in an entirely new light. If he'd been the one to assist she'd have been angry—she'd been angry even when she'd gotten to assist—but Ootaka wouldn't have had to give the admonition. Maybe she'd misjudged him.

She stepped in and leaned up on tiptoe, arms stretching toward his neck. A hug would be all right. He was a hugger. He came from a family of huggers… That's what normal people did. He'd hugged her that first day, and she'd been so thrown she hadn't really enjoyed it.

Slipping her arms around his shoulders, she pressed in close. For a second it seemed as if he might not hug her back, but then the firm warmth of his arms wrapped around her, complementing the strength and heat of his chest warming her.

She couldn't remember the last time someone had really hugged her. In the past couple of years people had always tried to touch her to convey support, but every touch had been gentle. Hugs that had been more air than substance. As if she was made of eggshells already riddled with cracks.

Enzo didn't do that. His arms around her felt solid and real. There was nothing between them, really—maybe friendship? But he held her as if she might get away from him if he loosened his grip. Everyone else's hugs felt more like…a cage of arms. Protective, maybe, but distancing. Lonely. *Cold.*

Somewhere in the back of her mind her promises echoed and bounced around. They always did, swirling and waiting for any sign of weakness to pounce. Janie hadn't had any hugs, be they cagey and cold or full of heat and… something else, some nameless want she didn't have time for and didn't deserve.

She should let go of him. But both arms stayed locked

around his shoulders, not ready to let go yet. Kimberlyn leaned back far enough to look into his eyes again so that if he looked troubled, that would give her motivation to put some air between them.

So blue, but that golden thread highlighting the pupils pulled her in like a miner with gold fever.

Her gaze drifted down over a nose with a slight crook around the bridge—speaking of fights in the past—to a sensual mouth framed by that scruff he wore so well. So close. Oh, man, was she going to kiss him?

The butterflies suddenly swarming in her stomach said yes. Yes, she was. Just one kiss.

The last thing she saw before closing her eyes was the surprise in his as her intention registered.

His head tilted to meet her. Warmth and gentle, firm pressure settled against her lips, a slow, leisurely kiss, as if he sensed that's what she needed.

In preparation for her transfer, her first year back in the residency program went by in a blur of studying, lingering physical therapy and work. She'd distanced herself from everyone, refusing any attempts others had made to improve her social life. Her education had become her everything. And that just couldn't change. Not yet. She'd promised Janie, or at least Janie's memory. Janie, the one who would never get to have another first kiss, or feel this desperation to get closer that Enzo's touches inspired in her.

The scent of strawberry lingered on his shirt, and the soft scrape of at least three days' growth of beard contrasted with all that was soft and sweet-smelling about him.

Her heart stuttered and sped up.

His hands slid down, kneading her hips and then cupping her backside. A lift, a turn, and she sat on the counter. He slipped between her legs and pulled her close against him, then his hands traveled back up to cup the back of her neck and deepen his kiss. Open mouths, stroking tongues, thundering hearts, breaths that came shallow and quick, and heat blooming between her legs where he'd pulled them together.

The anatomy of a perfect kiss. It was just kissing. Kissing was not naked stuff, no matter what her hips wanted. Kisses didn't constitute a relationship, but it warmed a cold, hollow place inside her.

Until his fingers pressed just a little more firmly where they curled under her jaw, and he broke the kiss to look down at her, his brows pinching. "You've got an irregular heartbeat..."

Her eyes came back into focus and she saw a frown in his.

Great, so now having someone cup her jaw could give everything away? He'd been feeling her carotid.

She leaned back swiftly, cracking the back of her head against the cabinet behind her. "It's okay. I'm okay." A couple of deep breaths and the fluttering feeling in her chest passed. "I get a little bit flip-floppy at times. It's nothing to worry about."

He leaned back just a touch more, though his hips still rested against the counter. "Is it A-fib?"

"Not sufficient for a diagnosis or medication," Kimberlyn whispered, adding, "It really only happens..." When she got excited. Something else she didn't want to admit. That might lead him to thinking this kissing business was more than a mistake...

"When your heart speeds up?" He grinned, showing how pleased he felt with himself for making her heart speed up.

"Yes." She breathed the word on a sigh.

"Consequences of the accident?"

"No." Another quick denial, as per protocol...

He lifted a brow, and might've well called her a liar out loud.

She tried again. "My heart's in good condition. It's really fine. A mild electrical issue from time to time."

"The cause?"

She shoved lightly at his chest, opening enough space to bring both legs to one side and slide down from the counter. There was probably some rule about using the counters for anything but food-related activities anyway. Once both feet were on the floor, she put some distance between them. "It's fine now. Steady and normal. Really, I don't need to be diagnosed or worried about. I run all the time, give it a good workout. It's not a problem."

Skeptical eyebrows stayed in place and suddenly the idea of him thinking it was because of the kiss sounded much better than the idea that she wasn't fit for the job or the fellowship…

"It happens when I get excited, okay? And you can just shut up about it, Mr. I'm-Kind-of-a-Jerk-but-the-Ladies-Don't-Mind-Because-I'm-a-Great-Kisser."

Yes, it happened when anything got her too excited. It had happened briefly at Mr. Elliot's accident—from fear that time, but the result was the same. And he didn't need to know that, either.

That smile returned and he snagged her arm to pull her back to him, closing up that gap she'd put between them. "Want me to kiss you again? A test to see if we can replicate conditions? I'm happy to do so."

"You're offering to kiss me just so you can monitor my pulse?" She rolled her eyes, shaking her head. "Oh, take me now, smooth talker."

"Actually, I was planning on monitoring your hips, or possibly inspecting the areas closer to your heart. They are…beckoning."

Kimberlyn lost any idea of whether they were fighting or flirting. "We were just arguing."

"But you kissed me and I came up with a cunning plan on getting information from you."

Enzo's hands stayed at her waist, holding her to him so she had to crane her neck to look up at him. "What's your plan?" She really shouldn't be encouraging him. A fling—

because it surely couldn't be anything else—was not part of her five-year plan. One day she might have that, and maybe a husband and children...when she deserved them. When she'd earned them by keeping her promises.

"I'll pay you in orgasms."

She laughed despite her mental reminders. "You're pretty confident. How do you know you could deliver?"

"Are you kidding?" he asked, hands kneading her hips as he slid her back to him. "I'm a master of anatomy. I know the female form intricately and have devoted at least half of my life—probably more like three-quarters—to observing it in its natural habitat."

There it was, the rascally charm she'd witnessed at dinner with his family, only naughtier alone with her. She flushed to the tops of her ears while a more insistent heat settled lower in her belly. It'd be inappropriate if they hadn't just been kissing a minute or two ago.

"You sound like you've been studying gorillas in the mists with Jane Goodall." She tried to sound grumpy. What she should be doing was putting space between them, but what actually happened was her sliding her arms around his waist and leaning her cheek against his chest. Dumb, but...it felt necessary.

He chuckled and leaned down to kiss the side of her neck, causing her pulse to soar.

How had this started? Oh, yeah, she'd kissed him.

A dang good decision. Or a really awful one. "I think you're making promises you don't know if you can keep."

"I didn't say they'd be your orgasms." Enzo kept up the flirty banter, his words tickling her neck. Coupled with the heat spreading through her limbs, if she didn't stop this soon...

She hadn't felt this good in such a long time. Which was probably how it should be, but it was hard to turn away from. Playful flirting almost left her feeling nostalgic. "So it'd just be orgasms in my honor?"

"Maybe. Maybe not." Leaning back, he looked her in the eye again, his face scant inches away. "I'd certainly do my best to make sure it was the other way, but I left some wiggle room in my wager so I can fulfill the letter of the agreement if you had any sort of performance issues."

"So there will be orgasms for someone, eh?" She should stop this. "It's somewhat less convincing that way."

But no less tempting.

Only she'd have to take off her clothes for sure then, and exposing the physical signs of trauma would expose the emotional traumas…and those were the ones that could really hurt her.

Right. That did it. She shoved against his chest until enough distance opened that she couldn't feel his heat through the air. The warmth of his arms around her, the firmness of the chest and shoulders beneath the black T-shirt, the deep kisses and playful banter had all felt too good.

It might have been better when she'd been viewing him as a viper out to ruin her.

It was going to be harder to compete now that she actually liked him.

CHAPTER SIX

ENZO STOOD AT his locker, changing into fresh scrubs, when Kimberlyn rushed in. The front of the light blue scrubs she wore were soaked in what he could only be a little envious of: in the rock-paper-scissors of viscous scrub splatter, blood always beat barf. And his scrubs, the ones he'd just removed? Barf City.

Her shoulders curled forward and she pinched the front of the scrub top, pulling the saturated fabric out to create a hollow at her chest—no doubt an attempt to keep the long-sleeved, white Spandex undershirt she always wore from becoming soaked, too.

Once inside the door, she whisked the blue top off, revealing the sanguine splatter saturating the white beneath.

Attempt unsuccessful.

Since their kiss Enzo hadn't seen much of her. Ootaka had been called in during the night a couple of times, which had meant that Enzo had been called in, too. It had messed up his schedule.

If he was honest, there was more to it than simple conflicting schedules. He hadn't really been avoiding her, as he did Lyons, but the urge to see her, flirt with her, hadn't diminished at all over the week. A week in which he'd had time to really consider the ramifications of kissing her. Or, more precisely, what could happen if he gave in to the urge to kiss her again.

He already had the urge to help her with Ootaka, already had the urge to protect her. And the way she'd clung to him when she'd hugged him might've stayed with him even more than the kiss.

After tossing her scrub top into the hamper for hazardous materials, Kimberlyn maneuvered in front of a mirror to look at her bloody chest again. Then at the sink. The paper towels. Weighing up...

She didn't want to take that top off, and he knew in an instant what that was about.

Scars. She'd seen both sides of the trauma table, and orthopedic surgeries weren't really what the trauma table was about. Surgeries to repair broken bones and torn ligaments waited until the life-threatening stuff had passed. So the trauma table would have dealt with the torso. Organs. Hemorrhages...

Something else that had been on his mind since the kiss in the kitchen—he wanted to know, and he also didn't want to know.

A nice guy would probably go somewhere else, let her keep her secrets, but Enzo wasn't feeling particularly nice.

As closed-lipped as she could be, if he stormed ahead and demanded to know exactly what he wanted, she wouldn't budge. Start small. Innocuous questions.

"Looks like you've been into something more exciting than barf basin patrol."

"Gunshot," she confirmed, her frown deepening as she stared back at the shirt.

Definitely more exciting. "With Ootaka?"

"No." She turned away from the mirror and frowned more deeply. "I can't wear this."

Not Ootaka, but still surgery trumped being the master of being puked on by sick children. "Are you going to jump in the shower? You really should get that cleaned off your skin. I could bring your fresh scrubs to you if you want."

The offer was another difficult one to make. His instincts were more wild man than civilized in certain situations—work and sex being right at the top.

Work meant the competition.

The competition meant there shouldn't be any sex. But sex was right at the top of his thoughts when her name or anything remotely related to her popped into his head.

And he wanted to see those damned scars. That was where his wild man went even more animalistic: Kimberlyn's scars might be where work and sex overlapped. Competition, concern and an inability to deal with not knowing something he wanted to know.

Not many people ever told him to stuff it when he asked a question, but Kimberlyn pretty much did. Half answers, diversions, while he wanted specifics, details. As much as he'd enjoyed the intimidating reputation he'd earned over the past four years, when she failed to trust him with this information that had been—and continued to be—very important to who she was, it really set his caveman off.

"I…" Her cheeks puffed and she looked toward the showers. "Yes. But the only undershirt I have in there… Well, I spilled my yummy mocha on it yesterday so I wore my spare and didn't take everything home to wash. It was late and I forgot…" Another puffed sigh and she rattled off the combination to her locker and dashed for the shower stalls.

By the time he'd gotten his shoes back on and gotten to her locker she was calling from the bay, "Enzo?"

"The combination isn't working," he called back, rotating the dial again and giving the thing a jerk. Nothing.

Oh, lucky. She'd have to come out…

She yelled the combination again, and Enzo repeated the numbers back as he worked the dial to the respective numbers. Two turns to the right, blah-blah-blah, number, number, number…

Nothing.

"It's not working," he called back.

Caveman or gentleman? Caveman would go to the shower and make her come out. Gentleman…would get her scrubs from the machine.

With a grunt, he grabbed an extra towel—as far as he was willing to go in the gentleman direction right now—and went to meet her at the shower.

The curtain still closed, the water turned off, and he could see her feet facing the curtain. She wanted to come out. And she really didn't want to come out.

"Are you sure you did it right?" she asked from behind the curtain. "Two turns to the right, one to the left, back to the right?"

"I'm sure," he said and then chuckled a little. "I know you think I'm sneaky—which I will admit is my fault after our first meeting—but I'm not that underhanded."

"You want to see my scars," she pointed out, still hidden behind the flimsy curtain.

That was true. Why bother denying it? "Yes, I do. Just to be clear, I also want to see the rest of you, but I'm not lying about the combination not working. I also promise that I was at the locker bearing your name on tape."

He thrust the towel through the side of the shower curtain farthest from her feet and felt cold, damp hands grabbing for it.

It would be so easy to jerk that curtain out of the way, but there wouldn't be a shred of honor in the act. Even his caveman had some restraints. "Do you want me to go get you a set from the machine?"

"They don't have the… I need the Spandex. The…"

Enzo filled in, "The undershirt you always wear."

"They don't have those," she muttered in between grunts as she wrestled with her towels. God, what was she doing in there?

"No, but they have the tops and the bottoms."

"And I have to wear something. This will teach me to put off doing something. I should keep two extra shirts…"

She sighed and gestured through the curtain to the bench. "My badge is in my shoes."

He retrieved the badge, verified that he knew what sizes to get for her and headed out. When he came back she had finished drying and had snagged a third towel to fashion herself some kind of towel outfit...top, skirt and some kind of wrap? Just how many freaking scars did the woman have?

Enzo laid the scrubs on the bench along with her badge and headed back out.

No scar-viewing yet. It had only been a couple of weeks. Needing to know only felt important... Her health seemed fine, aside from those skipped heartbeats. Knowing wasn't critical. Not knowing wouldn't kill anyone.

He paused at the door and looked back at her, transfixed by her neck-to-knees terry-cloth covering. "Whatever your scars are, I'm not going to use it against you, Mouse." He'd used the nickname again, but it had started to sound like an endearment even to him—which was why he probably should stop using it. "I can understand being worried about it, but it's not going to happen. The only kind of old injury I might think could impair your ability to treat patients would be located on your head or your neck."

"Neck?"

"As in spinal-cord damage that kept you from being able to control your arms. Or seizures. Narcolepsy. Something dangerous."

She nodded, but still didn't offer any big revelations despite the thoughtful frown that confirmed she'd heard him.

"I might be a bastard sometimes, but even a bastard has some lines he won't cross." It might only be a teaspoon of honor, but it mattered. "But if your hesitation is about some kind of body shame, get over it. Having to cover yourself from head to toe every day is no way to live your life. It's limiting. You don't swim, do you?"

"No," she answered, and for once the *no* didn't sound fueled by reaction—a different emotion echoed in her voice. She knew he was right, but she wasn't quite ready to change yet. "I'm working on it. I think it'll be better next year, after this is over and after they've faded."

The smallest fragment of information. An opening.

"How long ago were your procedures?"

"Eighteen months since the last one. But they've been fading more slowly than most people's I know. I don't know why. Maybe my collagen is extra-colorful."

Six months before she'd resumed her residency. Not much of a clue—nearly anything healed in that time. He managed not to ask how many procedures she'd had. She might answer him, but she wasn't going to give locations and reasons to him today.

Seemed like a condition a surgeon wouldn't suffer from—shame over surgical scars—but maybe it was something more. It was enough for today, even if he really wanted to know. Take it slow.

Maybe sooner if he worked a little of his magic to assure her some OR time with Ootaka in the near future.

"Are you heading to one of the ORs?"

"No. The other guy, not Ootaka, has the gunshot. I was just helping in the trauma room."

The other guy. Exactly how he thought of Langley— "the other guy." Not Ootaka. Only Ootaka really mattered in their universe.

"Langley." He supplied the name, then headed out. He'd already been too long off the floor; surely somewhere there was some vomiting child who needed a target…

No matter how much Enzo told himself that he should just get back on the floor, he still found himself loitering outside the locker room, waiting for her.

The locker room was coed and the residents changed clothing in front of one another all the time, but waiting for her in the room would've been too aggressive. She never changed in front of others. She'd likely have changed in the bathroom if the shower hadn't been necessary.

The door opened and he had to step away to keep from getting smacked by it.

Kimberlyn stepped out, her face pale and one hand plastered over the V-neckline of the scrub top, covering the skin.

"I… It's not very concealing," she whispered, and Enzo pulled his gaze from her hand to her eyes.

Scrubs were anything but revealing…

Hand over that part of her chest? It wasn't cleavage she was hiding. As nice as her curves were, they didn't make cleavage up to her clavicle. If she had a scar beneath her hand, it could only be for one reason.

He wrapped his fingers around the slender wrist and pulled her hand firmly away from her chest, revealing a cord of scar tissue tracking down the center of her chest. It looked even angrier than the one on her shoulder had.

"Your chest was cracked?"

He hadn't needed to ask the question. He knew already that it had been, but the idea that she had been injured so badly in her accident made something feel hollow and haunted inside him.

She looked away, swallowed and nodded.

Enzo wasn't really prone to randomly hugging people. Yes, his family was like that, and he hugged when it seemed like something a sibling or his mother needed. And he hugged Maya all the time because the first months of her life had been such a scary time, and during much of it she had been sequestered in an incubator, starved for contact.

But he'd never hugged another colleague.

He pulled open the door again and tugged Kimberlyn back into the relative privacy of the locker room.

As the door swung closed he tugged her into his arms and clutched her to his chest, as if having her there would relieve the sudden tightness there.

The thing was, she was right. This made him feel differently about her.

Not that she couldn't do the job.

Not that she was less than any of the other residents, not that she was handicapped at all...

The strength he hadn't questioned at the scene of Elliot's accident now seemed precious and transient. She felt dainty, but he knew her to be determined. Until then he'd never questioned her endurance. She looked completely fit with her clothes covering the scars.

Now she felt fragile. She felt to him the way Maya's tiny body felt—as if she could be snatched away by a strong breeze.

"I don't want to know what happened." The words croaked out before he'd even given them much thought.

His hoarse confession was further muffled by the instinct to press his nose into the hair at her crown.

"You don't?" she whispered back. Then tacked on, "Good."

Regular volume would have made this conversation worse somehow.

It also would've increased the chance that anyone who happened to come into the locker room might overhear them.

"Just...don't tell me right now." He swallowed, pulled back enough to look down into those dark, hurt eyes. "Not because I don't care." He pried his own arms from around her, trying to regain some ground. "It's just a lot for work."

A lot of emotion. A lot of worry. A lot of nothing he could even do to fix this situation. He couldn't change her past, whatever it was that had happened to her. He felt helpless, and he was a fixer, a protector...

"Bolt cutters." He blurted the words out as the thought came to him. "Stay here. If you get called, delay for a few minutes. I'll be right back."

Having seen the scar, at least he knew she'd been under

the care of a cardiologist to take care of whatever had happened. Someone had fixed her. Someone was keeping track of her, or had been before she'd moved north. If she said the irregular beats were nothing to worry about…if she was being honest with him…he should feel better about that.

Doing something would help. He hurried to Maintenance.

Kimberlyn watched Enzo leave while pulling at the back of her scrub top so that the V in the front inched up to her collarbone. Covered. As long as she didn't move. She sat on the bench in front of her locker.

He didn't want to know. That was strange. But good. For her. Maybe he'd stop asking questions now. He'd probably keep his distance, too. Definitely good for her that he felt that way.

So why did she feel as if she'd just lost something?

Clearly her priorities had become clouded.

He was helping her with the lock, which was certainly a victory. He had learned about the big scar and he was going to help her hide it. All good. She didn't even know where to get bolt cutters at the hospital.

Good things. Victories. The only way her week could be better was if Mr. Elliot regained consciousness. He'd been transferred to a care facility that morning, never having come round. They had taken him off the machines, and his lower brain function was enough to sustain him for now, but that could only go on for so long.

The highlight of her time in New York so far had been the weekend, the dinner with his family, and the kissing and flirting that now jockeyed with her guilt for control over her thoughts during any minutes her mind had time to wander.

Someone came in, greetings flew in passing and she moved to the other side of the room and sat again—kept sitting, kept waiting, kept quiet… Maybe anyone else coming into the locker room would stay on the other side of the locker wall divide and never know she was there.

Before she had to make excuses Enzo returned with the bolt cutters and headed for her locker. One loud crack announced the severing of one side of the lock, and then another and the body fell away.

She opened the door and dragged out the long-sleeved, white Spandex undershirt that was a necessary part of her uniform and whisked the other top off, not waiting for Enzo to leave.

He made no show of shielding his eyes or giving her privacy now. With the intensity of his gaze she was probably lucky he hadn't forcibly stripped her to look for the other scars. As she pulled the shirt over her head, he circled her, taking in every inch of flesh on display.

Thank goodness she'd not picked some lacy, sexy bra to wear today. It had been a sports bra day.

"Rotator cuff. Chest..." He listed two places that had needed to be repaired and then reached to touch the third scar on her belly. "What was this one?"

He could ask about that, but not about the heart. "It was a bit of metal."

"What did it hit?" he asked.

"Perforated the jejunum," she explained and heard him swear.

"Anything else where you're covered?"

"Broken left femur. Three screws."

"What happened?" he asked, then quickly followed it up with lifted palms. "No, don't tell me."

Someone from the door called to him, and he stepped that way, then right back. Indecision? She'd never have thought him possible of it.

"Tell me. And move your things to my locker." He gestured to her locker, which she'd now shut, lockless. A few quick turns of his combination lock and it came open. It figured that *his* lock would work.

"What if I need something today?"

"I'm going to give you the combination."

He had already dug out his notebook and pen and scribbled down the numbers.

She moved her things over, especially her bag and electronics…things she needed to not be stolen.

"You're not talking," he pointed out, tearing out the sheet with his combination and folding it once before he handed to her.

"It was a car wreck. We flipped. A couple of times."

"Hit other cars?"

"Hit a large piece of tire that flew off a tractor trailer on the highway, lost control and went off the side of the road into a… If I say the car went off a bridge, then it sounds like a big bridge over a huge river, which isn't accurate. It was a small bridge over a creek, mostly just bridging a gap between the banks…maybe about twenty-five feet across. The car didn't get all the way to the water, just to the bank leading down."

She pinched the fabric of her pants between thumb and index finger, then slid the material back and forth. Something physical to focus on. That coping mechanism was how she kept from being sucked back to the scene anytime she had to talk about it. Sometimes the physical focus was more vigorous than just worrying the fabric to make scraping sounds. Sometimes she had to pinch herself…or dig her nails in until she left tiny, half-moon bruises.

He was too quiet, but it was a heavy sort of quiet.

"Please, don't hug me again right now." She was definitely going to cry if she got hugged right now, and that wouldn't help her terrible day at all.

His phone beeped and he reached for it, then turned away to answer it, giving her the perfect window for escape.

She slipped out the door while he spoke in short, clipped tones to whatever angel had interrupted.

* * *

Kimberlyn spotted her lunch date across the crowded cafeteria and made a beeline for Tessa's table in the corner. Out of deference to Kimberlyn, Tessa had chosen the table with the best view of the room, and one that also gave the most privacy.

She set her tray on the table and dropped into the seat opposite. "I don't have a lot of time, but I needed to see someone uncomplicated."

Tessa grinned, "I don't know that I've ever been called that, but I like it that you think so."

"You're not Enzo. And you're not Ootaka. And that's about the limit of my brainpower to make comparisons right now. I called Mr. Elliot's facility to check on him again today. They're going to think that I'm the worst doctor in history, but I keep hoping that the upper level brain function will return. Stupid, right?"

"Not stupid, but maybe the hope would be better spent somewhere else."

Something that Kimberlyn appreciated about Tessa, she was warm and kind. She felt like someone from back home, as if they could have been friends for ages or gone to high school together. It was no wonder to Kimberlyn that Caren and Tessa were close. With her cousin out of the country, Tessa had become the closest confidante she had.

"I know you're right. I know talk of miracles is usually looked at askance in our occupation, but unexplained recoveries happen. I guess I just feel like…why was I the one on scene with him—me who recognized his symptoms and such—if I wasn't supposed to save him? It's just upsetting."

Tessa nodded. "Wish I had an answer for that."

She knew a little more about Kimberlyn's history through Caren and their discussions prior to her move, but she didn't know everything. And Kimberlyn didn't have the heart to talk about that right now, either. The words always scalded her tongue coming out. They were the kind of words best kept bottled.

"There's number one, Dr. Complicated." She nodded to Enzo, grabbing coffee instead.

"What's going on with Enzo?"

"I don't know. Stuff. Nothing. He confuses me, too. And I don't think he ran off those other residents." She lowered her voice. "I think Ootaka did."

Tessa's brows shot up and she leaned in to keep the conversation quiet. "Why would he do that?"

"Not on purpose. But you know his big list of guidelines for the type of behavior and decorum that best serves a surgeon in and out of the operating room?"

Tessa nodded.

"Well, you can't tell anyone this. It's just Enzo's theory—which he actually shared with me—but I think he's onto something. We think that if you violate Ootaka's guidelines in his OR, he just stops inviting you to assist. Now, during the fifth year, there are very few old trauma residents who get to practice with him. Enzo is mostly it. And I haven't been invited back into the OR since my first day with Mr. Elliot.

"Which apparently is because I wasn't...forceful or commanding enough? That leadership thing he has? I didn't do it well enough on my first day. Still not sure how I was supposed to be leading him, and really that first week was kind of crazy for me, trying to figure out how everyone liked to work...but my deference made me seem wishy-washy. He's not invited me back."

"So you think people are just realizing that they are not going to be in the running for his fellowship and transferring out?"

"I think so. One went to Cardiothoracic, right? And I want to say that the other one just decided to stick with general surgery without additional training after."

"Right." Tessa leaned back, her shoulders lifting slightly

as she considered what Kimberlyn had shared. "So Enzo told you this? That doesn't seem like him, either."

"I think he's got image issues and he lets them perpetuate so people are a little bit intimidated by him. He's not really a bad guy. He's kind of blunt and aggressive at times and, yes, he is arrogant as heck, but he's not blindly mean. He just doesn't really curb his tongue when he's got something to say. But you should see him with his family. He's completely different."

"You like him?"

Kimberlyn sighed. "Yes." It was only a month or so into the year and she had a big whopping crush on her competition. Mortifying. "You should see him with his baby niece. It's just so unfair. I don't know what it is about big handsome men carrying babies around. They might as well make that illegal. It's as potent as a drug." She remembered that she was supposed to be eating and set about remedying that with her broiled salmon and steamed veggies.

Tessa's knowing look compelled her to continue talking. "It doesn't really matter if I like him, but maybe it's a good thing. We've come to some kind of unspoken agreement that we'll fight fair up until January, when Ootaka makes the announcement." Yep, if it sounded like stupid reasoning to her own ears, she could only imagine how it sounded to Tessa. "And then one of us will have to chop the head off the other one and absorb all his power, just like on *Highlander*."

"Should've saved that zinger for Sam."

"Enzo's probably more likely to have seen it." And he liked to joke. And flirt. And...darn, she really did like him.

Kimberlyn stabbed a bunch of broccoli on her fork and shoveled it into her mouth.

Why couldn't he actually have been a jerk to her? Her life was complicated enough without adding something else to feel guilty about. If she gave in to temptation, that meant giving him time. Time she should be spending studying or observing surgeries from the gallery suites.

She should never have gone to that house, met his family or seen him with that baby...

CHAPTER SEVEN

A RINGING PHONE woke Kimberlyn about three hours into the thirty hours of sleep she really wanted.

Fifteen minutes later, she was up, teeth and hair brushed, standing at the foot of the brownstone stairs, waiting for Enzo.

When all hands were called in for surgery in the middle of the night, something big was happening. Something big meant Ootaka would be involved. Something big with Ootaka meant she might get to impress him more than she apparently hadn't impressed him on her first day, if Enzo was right.

Enzo pulled up in his sporty black something or other just as she scrubbed her face with the emergency cleansing cloths she kept on hand for the times when she slept in the on-call room, or got called from sleep and emergency hygiene conditions were a thing.

No makeup at all today. She didn't usually load up with the stuff, but she liked it when her eyelashes had some semblance of a presence. Men did it without mascara, a grossly unfair cosmic irony, and she'd actually spent time looking for the reason in medical texts in the past…because every question needed an answer.

"Morning," he said as she climbed in.

"It's not morning. It's two—"

"In the morning," he finished.

She buckled in and stuffed the used cloth into her bag. The last thing she wanted to do was to primp in front of the man, though that mirror she knew would be atop the sun visor tempted her with the siren song of her mascara wand...

No. She'd already been neurotic enough about her appearance in front of him. Besides, something big was going on at the hospital so no one was going to notice or care that she was not well put together at 2:00-freaking-a.m.

"Do you know what is going on? I didn't get a chance to ask when they called in." Or maybe she hadn't had the brainpower to form words in the fifteen seconds after waking when she had been listening on the phone.

"Organ harvest," Enzo said, working through the gears as he got the vehicle up to speed...and maybe a little past the speed limit.

"Was it someone who just came in tonight?"

Enzo shrugged, then mumbled, "I don't know. I didn't ask who the donor was."

Something else he didn't want to know? Just as he hadn't wanted her to tell him what they'd been treating when they'd cracked her chest?

Well, she wanted to know, and prayed it wasn't one of her patients.

At least it wasn't Elliot, he'd been gone from the hospital for a couple of weeks. She laid her head back, closing her eyes. Enzo was the one driving. She didn't need to think or take responsibility for anything right now, and sometimes she needed that space.

By the time they arrived Ootaka was already talking to the group of residents he'd pulled in to get ready.

As with everything, Ootaka had a very well-organized manner of conducting harvests. Their patient was a DNR who'd been revived enough to sustain life, no doubt with machines. A cadaver with a heartbeat, folks liked to say.

Appropriate and inappropriate at the same time. Also, something she'd never been involved with before.

Since it was up to him to orchestrate the harvest, Ootaka used the trauma residents first. Enzo was given the liver to assist with removal and readying for transport. She was given the kidneys. Lungs to a third resident... with the heart coming last before another surgical team swapped in to recover tissues that could be taken after the heart was removed.

She got the second spot. That had to be worth something. Maybe Ootaka's opinion of her wasn't so bad. Maybe he just hadn't had a surgery he'd wanted her in on before. She could still be competition.

Or maybe she was just the most favored of those rejected from Ootaka's OR.

Enzo and Ootaka worked in tandem to get the donor onto the heart bypass pump before removing the liver. While he worked, she was tagged to scrub in so she'd be ready when Ootaka was. When she was at the table, the third resident would scrub in to be ready to remove lungs, and so on.

As she dragged the brush over her nails and creases in the fingers where bacteria might congregate, she watched through the glass partition separating the scrub room from the surgery going on.

She'd not been given the opportunity to watch Enzo perform much yet, and while her vantage point wasn't the greatest from the scrub room, she could see the concentration in the furrow of his brow, or at least the way it bunched under his scrub cap and the careful, confident way he moved and anticipated Ootaka.

When Enzo had shared his theory she'd doubted him a little. Not his concern, not the fact that he had been being honest with her—it hadn't been an act to throw her off—but she'd figured that warning her after one surgery with one small correction had been overestimating the importance of the guidelines. But today was the first time she'd been invited back, and that probably wouldn't have even happened if it hadn't been for the all-hands nature of the procedure.

She scrubbed more vigorously. Get done, get all the nooks and crannies and then get out there where she could better see and hear how the two men operated, and the way they complemented one another during the procedure. There could be no better instruction than witnessing what Ootaka would consider a well-orchestrated surgery. Who knew if she'd have another chance to try to dazzle after this?

She stomped on the sink pedal to turn off the water and headed out to the nurse to get gowned and gloved, then moved into position where she could see but didn't crowd. The patient's head was suddenly visible to her and a wave of cold prickles washed over her face and down her chest to where her heart stuttered in that way it liked to do when she was hit with a boost of adrenaline...

"Mr. Elliot," she whispered his name.

Enzo looked over at her briefly, letting her know with just a glance that he was right there with her. And that she'd said the name out loud.

A display of emotion in Ootaka's OR. She clamped her mouth shut and tried to focus.

She knew the ethics of all organ harvests and had read about the steps taken to vet a potential donor, the therapies required for the family, diseases and infections to be screened for...

She just hadn't known all that could happen without her knowing about it. It had only been a day or two since her last call to the care facility to check up on him. No one had said anything, but maybe he hadn't been through the screening then? Or maybe no one had told her because... he wasn't really her patient anymore. She was just the doctor who called more than was acceptable, the doctor who couldn't let go.

She'd known he'd had limited brain function after the accident. His body had sustained itself, but there had been no upper-level function. He'd just stayed alive. And in that condition, without a "Do Not Resuscitate" order, the family could've left him with a feeding tube in a care facility indefinitely.

Something she'd been purposefully not thinking about. She hadn't wanted him to die, but she hadn't wanted others to suffer or harbor the impossible hope that he'd wake up. She'd avoided thinking about the whole situation, avoided talking much about him...

If she wanted to get through this surgery with her professional decorum intact, she needed to continue not thinking about the fact that the man they'd worked so hard to save her first day was physically dying today. Another phase of the denial she'd been going through since the man had failed to regain consciousness in Post-op that day.

Pay attention to Enzo, the way he worked to augment Ootaka's actions and anticipate them. The removal of the liver ended with a tray and Enzo off to another area of the operating room to prepare it for transport.

As soon as he stepped away, she stepped in, breathing through her nose slowly and deeply. Controlling her emotions began with controlling her physical reactions to them. Deep breathing kept her heart rate more or less even.

"I'm glad you made it in tonight, Dr. Davis," Ootaka said to her, meeting her eyes over the donor. "We will give him a chance to help others. It is fitting that we do so together, yes?"

She swallowed and nodded, "Yes, Doctor. I want to be able to do what's best for him." And if helping get his organs to others was the only way to keep him alive in some small way, that's how she would do what was best for him.

Even if it meant disconnecting from the whole damned situation to get it done.

She offered a number twenty-two scalpel to Ootaka and when he took it she grabbed clamps and got ready to do what was needed. Anticipate. Be certain when she ordered the associate staff to do something. Make decisions, don't seem uncertain…

Don't think about Mr. Elliot until later.

After the liver left his care, Enzo retired to the lounge so he could suck down as much coffee as they'd let him have.

Heck of a morning.

And Kimberlyn's eyes when she'd realized who the donor was…

He'd hoped she wouldn't, but the bruising and the freshly healing incision on the man's chest had assured she would. Even if his face had been concealed, she would've known.

He could only pray that it wouldn't affect her performance with Ootaka. When she'd said Elliot's name, Ootaka had given no indication that he'd heard her.

Two kidneys to remove, twice as much time needed. She would be in there longer than he had. Her physical endurance wasn't a question for him—it wasn't that long a procedure—but her emotional endurance? That was the wild card today.

His phone buzzed and he fished it out of the pocket on his thigh.

Transplantation of kidney at seven. You're assisting.

The number was one he didn't recognize, so he thumbed through the numbers to find Langley. Not his number. He tried a few other guesses, a growing sense of dread filling his middle as he found and eliminated number after number.

If it was Lyons…no way was Enzo assisting.

A few more calls and he'd reached the answering service for Lyons's practice...and confirmed that the number
did indeed belong to his father.

Perfect. The only way to make this god-awful morning worse.

He hadn't spoken directly to his father since right after
the high-school graduation he'd failed to attend...so Enzo
texted back.

Not interested.

There. He'd responded without any swearing or name-
calling.

He slammed back the coffee and went to get a refill.
When he'd sucked that one down, too, he texted Kimberlyn.

Find me when your surgery is done.

He could do that at least, check on her. And she'd probably want to know that one of Elliot's kidneys was going
to a recipient today. Even if he wanted nothing to do with
the surgery or the surgeon, she probably would.

Besides, even if he was in the running for World's Worst
Sperm Donor, Lyons was an exceptional surgeon—a large
part of the reason Enzo would sooner carve out his own
spleen with a broken spork than let his father come anywhere near his career. He'd gotten this far on his own, and
when he got where he was going he wanted no one to be
able to even hint that he'd done so by riding coattails.

She didn't need to know that garbage. But witnessing
the transplant would be a good opportunity for her. Sometime over the past couple of weeks, since he'd discovered
much of what she'd overcome on her way to the current
fellowship, he'd stopped wanting to win at all costs. Oh,
he still wanted the fellowship. He just also wanted to pre-

serve a friendship with her. It wasn't pity, and it wasn't wholly attraction, either—though that played a part in it, he'd have to admit...

He'd just found a line he wouldn't cross to get it. Another line, rather. The Lyons line had been established long ago, but if he had to cut Kimberlyn down in any way to get there, he didn't know that he could do it, either. That included sabotaging her. She could gain something from assisting, and she also deserved it. It might even help her deal with Elliot's death.

He texted Ootaka to suggest that the trauma surgeon recommend Kimberlyn to assist his father in his stead.

CHAPTER EIGHT

"I DID THIS without your support or your money, and I'm going to finish it the same way. I don't need your help. I don't need your current suspicious favoritism. I don't need you."

Kimberlyn stopped dead in her tracks, hearing Enzo's raised voice around the corner of one of the long basement hallways peopled by staff and generally only patients en route to and from the surgical suites. Raw, undisguised disgust turned his tone to acid. No matter how blunt she knew he could be in his opinions, she'd never actually heard anger in his voice before.

Had they heard her walking? Who was Enzo fighting with? He'd wanted her to come find him...

Ootaka's voice reached her ears next, loud enough to recognize, not loud enough to hear the words.

Was he *yelling* at Ootaka?

Even if he wasn't, Ootaka would be unhappy to find Enzo yelling at anyone. That would clash with his mission statement of making an Ootaka ditto...one without displays of emotion.

She peeked around the corner, as unable to keep from doing so as she was to keep her heart in perpetual rhythm.

No, another man. Silvery-blond hair. Green scrubs. Fair. Trim and athletic.

Exact same stature as Enzo.

Seeing movement, Enzo looked toward her and gestured her toward them. "Here, this is Dr. Davis. She was
the one who saved Elliot on the scene, making certain he
lived long enough to get to the hospital in the first place.
There'd be no kidneys harvested for your lifesaving oper-
ation if it weren't for her. She also assisted in harvesting
the kidneys. She's the one who should be assisting you."

Her feet refused to obey. Instead of purposeful walking,
she tracked forward slowly with no sudden movements.
The same way she might approach—or creep past—an
angry canine.

Should she shake the man's hand? What was the proper
reaction when there was yelling? Kimberlyn grinned without showing teeth as she approached. Habit.

The unidentified surgeon looked toward her and her
heart kicked again. Deep blue eyes. She took a couple more
steps forward, needing to verify what instinct was telling her: that there'd be a matching thread of gold running
through them, just like in Enzo's hazel blues.

"I'm sure Dr. Davis is a fine surgeon, but the invitation
was specially for you," the man said, turning his attention
back to Enzo.

Father. She'd lay money on it. His golden looks didn't
mesh at all, but the stature…and those eyes… Someone
not obsessed with them might not even notice.

Her feet stopped moving about five feet away. Should
she approach further? Should she leave? Family drama,
in public… But at least it was only the four of them in the
hallway. Maybe this scene wouldn't go any further if no
one else happened by, though gossip spread like an infec-
tious disease within the close confines of the hospital. Enzo
might not care if anyone heard him giving his father the
finger, but the man already had gossip dedicated to him
that he liked and rarely let people see anything deeper.

"So considerate of you." Sarcasm dripped from Enzo's
words as he laid a hand over his heart. "Don't extend me

any more special invitations. I prefer the old universe where I pretend you don't exist and you pretend that we don't."

We. Family. Not just him... From what she'd seen of him with his family, she'd wager that the pronoun selected hadn't been accidental. Enzo might've been able to forgive if his gripe was just about him, but it was about "we"...

Enzo headed for her, and as he passed he took her hand so that she was forced to spin and scramble after him, off down the hallway, with his long, purposeful strides eating up the distance.

She heard Ootaka backing Enzo's suggestion about her, but Enzo wanted to get out of there and he apparently wanted her to be with him. So she went. He wanted her with him, and that was enough. She would've gone even without witnessing that bitter display.

After the ache she'd been feeling in her chest since she'd realized it had been Mr. Elliot on the table she'd needed to see Enzo, too. It had been a relief to come out of the OR to his text.

And now there were even more messy emotions in the mix.

"Is that your dad?" she asked as he tugged her through a door into the stairwell and beneath the flight leading up.

"He's not my dad. He's my father. I told you, Ernst Marino was my dad. Don't let your tender heart feel sorry for Lyons. He's got everything else he wants."

Her back touched the cool brick wall behind her and he pressed in against her, his free hand capturing her cheek as he leaned in.

His kiss came without any other preamble, no flirty dance up to the heat, no real warning—unless having her hand held for the first time in two weeks and being half dragged down a hallway by an angry, glowering man counted as a warning.

This wasn't about her. He wanted to blot out the earlier exchange, and she was there. Not a relationship. Not a danger to her five-year plan, either. Janie would have said that she was acting stupidly, all these rules shutting down her emotions and possibilities in life. Caren said it, too. The plan that had been so clear before had become clouded with Enzo in the picture.

The hand that held hers turned to slide his fingers between hers, hot palms melding together the way his hips pressed into her. He was claiming more from her than a salve in the form of kisses.

She'd object if she didn't need him, too. They were alive. She was alive. It might not be right that she was here and Janie was not, but suffering alone would never bring her friend back. The rasp of his stubble against her lips only made his kisses sweeter.

Something had already changed in the way she thought about him and the situation. The guilt she felt for giving in to temptation had even started to slack off.

Her free arm slid around his shoulders, where she could knead the corded muscles in the back of his neck, anchoring him to her, keeping him close. Firmness, strong shoulders and lean hips, heat and strength holding her against the hard wall.

The other time he'd kissed her it had been playful and full of teasing. Passion contained, hinted at but not explored. But this was raw and full of need.

Coffee and spice, and not a hint of the bitterness she'd heard moments before in his voice and his words. And she needed this. She needed to touch, to feel connected to someone... They both needed this sweetness.

If he could make her feel better, that should help her stay on course. Just as long as she didn't get comfortable. Maybe if they both acknowledged their connection as being of a transitory nature, one meant to serve some higher purpose, then that might be okay.

Except Enzo didn't seem to be all that torn about a desire to spend time together.

She'd been asked out once since her accident and had agreed without thinking it through, but before they'd gone out the neckline of her shirt had gaped open, he'd seen the incision and had gone running the other way. People got involved with an eye toward the future, and someone who'd had open-heart surgery before thirty might not have much of a future. Even if the man hadn't been looking for marriage, it had still spoken of activity-limiting illness. Since then she'd counted out the prospect of dating or getting close to anyone. After the scars faded, she'd told herself. After she got through her residency. After she'd finished her fellowship. After she'd kept her promise.

After she deserved happiness.

And Enzo hadn't wanted to know. So in the back of his mind he must be thinking the same sort of thing: that knowing what had happened, and what her future might look like...limited things. But, God help her, she still wanted him in a way that made ignoring logic so easy.

Slow, deep kisses could blot out logic. Blot out the sadness she knew he shared at Mr. Elliot's passing—and further deepened their connection. If it helped him get through the years of hurt and apparent neglect from his father still lingering with him, or temporarily soothed the ache in her chest that never really went away, no matter how well-healed the bone and tissue beneath the still-red stripe...it had to be a good thing, on some level.

She didn't care that he wanted to live in denial where she was concerned. It meant that he wanted to be with her at least for today. Maybe he saw no future—really, could she see a future, either? One of them—probably him—would get Ootaka's fellowship and that was a special, one-person deal. She'd have to move on, probably to another city. Learn another new hospital and be one of a few in a less special fellowship where she'd still learn enough to do the job she was called to.

At the end of the year they'd go their separate ways and probably never see one another again.

That was reality. That was the future, regardless of her health or long-term prognosis.

She threaded her fingers through his silky black hair and clung tighter, feeding bad feelings into the furnace his kisses stoked low in her belly.

Just for right now. Just to get through.

Since no one but Enzo had been invited to assist in the transplant, Kimberlyn sat with a small number of other residents in the gallery to observe. Enzo was not among them. After he'd kissed her to the point of frenzy he'd urged her to watch the transplant and had left her gasping beneath the stairs...

Rather than give the impression that he cared even a tiny bit, he'd deny himself the experience of watching a transplant.

Pride was one of the seven deadly sins for a reason. It did his father no real harm for Enzo to miss this. If he truly cared about his Brooklyn children as little as he seemed to, then it wouldn't matter one bit to him if he drove his son away from something that would be to his benefit.

The problem was she cared. Things were so confused between them, but if she knew nothing else she knew that this was just a symptom of the big, angry, father-shaped scar he was hiding. She hid scars all the time.

Phone held in her lap, she watched through the window to the scene below, her fingers tapping the edge with the itch to summon him. Get him here... Or just maybe make him feel better somehow. A burden shared and all that.

Caving, she woke her phone and texted.

You should come sit with me in the gallery. We can do a running commentary on his technique.

Less than a minute later, he sent back: Wouldn't be fun if others got to witness my family drama.

We'll whisper. I'll start… You call that a functioning sub-cuticular knot? My mamaw could do better w/ a sewing needle and she's half-blind!

Pretending that she was fine was a stepping stone across the gully of *not fine*. Flirty banter with Enzo? Fun and less traumatizing than thinking about Mr. Elliot's passing and the tissue recovery still going on with the second surgical team.

It also kept her from examining why Enzo had put her name forward to assist, even if his father had declined his advice.

Ha-ha. He's already stitching?

No. I lied. I can do that so you'll fail when Ootaka gives us a pop quiz on the procedure. I'LL WIN.

He doesn't do pop quizzes. This isn't high school.

Fine. I'll do sports commentator then. No! Chess commentator! Nasal voice "It seems he's selected a number twenty-two scalpel. Let's see how his opponent deals with his opening…"

Who's the opponent?

His patient. Duh.

How's his opponent handling it?

It seems his patient has gone for some impressive obfuscatory technique to up the difficulty of this classic opening gambit!

Which means?

Blood. Duh.

I suck at this.

She smiled at the phone. He wouldn't play along with her if it wasn't helping at least a little.

I noticed.

I can't believe you texted the word obfuscatory.

I have mad tiny device typing skills.

I noticed.

He's going heterotopic, looks like.

Where?

Cradle of the pelvis.

It had been a surprise to her in medical school that transplanted organs didn't have to be planted in a mirrored position to where they'd been extracted from. She'd heard of the technique, but this was the first transplant Kimberlyn had ever witnessed. And considering the way he loathed his father, she imagined that Enzo hadn't witnessed any, either.

Well, she didn't want him to miss it. She also didn't want to appear weird and clingy with all the texting.

His silence spoke volumes.

Minutes ticked by and she texted again.

Did you fall asleep?

No. Just in a bad mood.

You should come up. Everyone's tired and leaving... Plus totally great way to flip BD the metaphorical finger. You still get to learn and you've made it clear you don't need his stupid overtures.

BD?

Bad Dad.

BF. And I'll pass.

Bad Father. God, she had to break that habit. His mother's second husband was the one who deserved the honor of the title *Dad*. Last time that mistake would happen. It was obviously important to him, the distinction between words.

What else are you doing that's better?

Lying in the on-call room.

You're in bed?

Yes.

Alone?

Yes.

Did I mention that transplants turn me on?

As soon as she hit Send she regretted it. They may have just been making out under the stairs, and they may have that other time, too, but there had been a long spell in between. She could just be a way to alleviate boredom.

No. She was more than that. He wanted her, even if he didn't want to want her. She just wasn't used to making such obvious moves...

I'll bribe you with orgasms.

Ahh, a strong bargaining position.

Don't you want to ask whose orgasms?

No. I'm good with them being yours as long as I get to participate. Or watch.

Heat flooded her cheeks. Was there anyone else in the gallery? She looked around to make sure she was, in fact, alone. The last observer had slipped out sometime since she had started texting...

You're taking me seriously? I may need some convincing to follow through.

Picture me naked. You've seen most of me already.

Yes, I have! It was nice.

Nice?!

I mean it was the BEST THING EVER. Are you coming now?

Coming? We haven't even started yet.

CHAPTER NINE

JUST AS THE KIDNEY was placed into the newly created spot, Enzo made it to the gallery.

Kimberlyn smiled when she saw him, stashed the phone she'd been texting with and sat up a little straighter.

True to her word, the gallery was empty.

He sat beside her and wrapped an arm around her shoulders, giving in to impulse simply because she felt good to touch.

"I'm glad you came." She snuggled in a little, taking comfort from him, as well.

That should have gotten him there sooner. The sadness he'd seen in her eyes during the organ recovery hadn't gone anywhere. She was just doing a good job of hiding it from most people. Including him, with the act she'd put on that had been all flirty and fun in the gallery. That had been for his benefit, to tempt him there.

He let his hand curl over her small shoulder, and against the hollow of his palm he could feel the scar from her rotator cuff surgery.

That wasn't a fun surgery, either, if any surgery could be called fun for the patient. But the shoulder was a painful thing when it healed. He couldn't imagine having that alongside a broken femur on the same side, a broken sternum from having his chest cracked and a bowel perforation.

She might feel delicate and fragile to him—and no doubt

she was more fragile now than she once had been—but she had to have been strong to make it through that and dive right back into her training.

Most people would have opted for an easier path after that kind of physical trauma, but she'd picked the hardest one she could find.

"Did you choose trauma because of your accident?" He still couldn't bring himself to ask what had meant her chest be cracked. He had the vague idea that the reason symptoms of cardiac tamponade had been etched on her brain was because she'd been diagnosed with the same at her accident. The same as the patient they'd officially lost this morning.

She nodded. "My primary surgeon was one of Ootaka's."

"Your trauma surgeon in Nashville was one of Ootaka's fellows?"

She nodded again. "One of his first, before he completed the last fellowship, the vascular specialty, and became the god of trauma surgery."

All trauma surgeons started out as general surgeons, which was what surgical residency was about. They went on to fellowships in trauma and critical care. Most stopped there, with licensing and practice.

Ootaka had gone on to several other fellowships—thoracic, cardiac and vascular. And all those would have come in handy when treating Kimberlyn.

Learning from Ootaka wasn't the same as obtaining all four separate fellowships, but it was the next best thing. Ootaka's fellows could go anywhere they wanted with the one fellowship.

He could see why she wanted it.

"I need to ask you a question, and I don't want you to get mad."

Enzo pulled his gaze from the surgery table—not that he had actually absorbed anything he'd been seeing the past several minutes. "Why would I get mad at a question?"

"Because it's to do with him, BF." She gestured with a flick of her finger to his father.

Enzo nodded for her to continue.

Her voice became quiet, gentle even. "What if he invited you to assist him as an overture to building a relationship?"

The question he'd been trying to ignore since the showdown.

"I'm sure it was," he said after the urge to shout settled down again. After the shouting match in the corridor, every time he opened his mouth he wanted to yell. But Kimberlyn didn't deserve his wrath. "But I still don't give a damn. I spent years seeking his approval, or even proof that he gave half a damn about me and my sisters. If he wants a relationship now, why isn't he also reaching out to them? Why didn't he even come by the hospital or send flowers when his first grandchild was in the NICU? Because he knew she was there. I guarantee he knew."

It was a good thing that the gallery was nearly deserted as his volume had started creeping up again at the end. It was even harder to moderate when speaking about Lyons's actions, or lack of actions. And it burned him even more that the only one of his children Lyons deigned to acknowledge was the male, and the surgeon. What about his little sisters? What about tiny Maya? How could he not want to know about his granddaughter?

"How did that happen? Why did they split up?" She watched the window, but Enzo could see that she was actually watching his reflection rather than the procedure below. Indirectly, probably so he didn't feel stared at.

"Lyons walked out on us when I was four. Mom, Sophia, Beth and me. Because he was tired of slumming it in Brooklyn."

"Slumming it?"

"He's Manhattan royalty. We're Brooklyn trash."

She scowled, angry on his behalf and apparently still unsure what to think. Her gaze tracked back through the glass to the surgeon below, her soft lips drawn into a flat, tight line. "And his name is Lyons. But your name is Della-Toro, and your mom and siblings are all Marinos. Where did DellaToro come from?"

That he could smile about. "Mom's maiden name is DellaToro. I filed for the name change on my eighteenth birthday. By then, she'd remarried Ernst, and you have met the second wave of siblings. He was a good man and we have a big happy family because of him. Ernst was the one who taught me how to be a good son, how to be a good brother."

"Good uncle," she said softly, the praise making him smile a little. "But you didn't take his name."

Enzo shook his head. "I wanted a blood tie with my name, and, as much as I loved Ernst and my younger siblings, Marino wasn't a name I felt ownership of."

All this talk about his last name reminded Kimberlyn of her words that first day. She looked directly up at him. "I'm sorry I said it was missing a word." She'd really been hateful to say that. The memory of the words rose like bile in her throat.

A quick head shake told her not to worry about it, but when he kissed her temple, it drove the sentiment home. Don't worry. About that. The arm around her shoulders loosened as his fingers tracked to the high, round neckline of her undershirt and then directly under it. He traced the scar on her sternum like braille that could tell him something he didn't want to ask.

Logically, she knew that the nerve endings in that seam had been severed and now no longer functioned. Since her sternum had healed beneath, there hadn't been any pain from touching it or pressure of any kind. No pain because there was no sensation.

That meant that every time it burned, the sensation was entirely in her mind. Knowing that didn't stop it from burning. Just like knowing there could be no sensation now didn't stop the rush of heat tracking over her chest and down her arms. Didn't stop the effervescent cascade from the imagined friction of his fingers on the tortured flesh anyone else would have avoided touching... No one but her and her doctors had ever touched it.

When she shivered, he looked down at her.

Did her cheeks glow as they felt they did? Had her pupils dilated with her faster breathing and heart rate? Desire had a very specific look, and this close... The look in his eyes confirmed it.

It was a familiar, intimate touch. His hands were soft, and the stroke of his long fingers so gentle. Tender even. Though they firmed in an exploratory way...

He was going to ask.

"Enzo..."

"I still don't want to know," he said quickly, withdrawing his fingers and curling her more firmly against his side, his gaze fixing once more on the gallery window. "You know, the name's not even really DellaToro." His voice rasped but gained strength as he spoke. "Mom's grandfather was a DellaTorre when he came through Ellis Island. DellaToro was a transcription error from Immigration."

He didn't want to know. Bad typists at Ellis Island had changed his name.

Who cared? Kimberlyn didn't even really want to stay and watch the surgery anymore. She was even having a hard time remembering why she should avoid those feelings. But God help her if she was going to pretend. She couldn't shrug it off as he did. "Torre means?"

"Tower."

She looked at him again, watched the corner of his jaw bunch and relax as he paused. No quick, easy flirting now. At least summoning words was hard for him, too.

"But he was a tiny man, preferred the idea of being linked with a bull... And ran with it. Remade himself into what he wanted to be."

She could see that trait as being inherited. Enzo came

from a blue-collar background and was intent and focused on reaching the top without help from someone who could've honestly done a lot to help his son if both—or either—of them had been so inclined.

She could use some of that strength of will right now.

Thinking about this, learning about him…it had all gone wrong somehow. Once he'd become more than a competitor, it felt as if every day she was coming up with a new way to cheerlead herself into some semblance of a belief that she could still prevail. That she still even wanted to. Because Enzo wasn't just a man on a personal mission, he was motivated for his whole family. It was noble. He actually was one of the good people she just pretended to be.

And maybe more deserving of the fellowship than someone just trying to clear bad debt from her moral ledger.

The mental back and forth exhausted her already overworked mind and heart. Something was going to happen between them, and she was going to let it. Because she wanted to. Because she was tired. Because she hurt, and somehow she hurt a little less those brief periods when she let his face block out Janie's.

"Look, he's tying it into the iliac and renal arteries rather than the aorta," Enzo said.

She laid her head against his shoulder because it hid her face and the tears suddenly threatening. The transplant was easier to talk about so she went with it. "Be harder to tap the aorta there. BF must have had some good vascular training, too."

Her parents weren't the most present people in the world, but they would never abandon her.

His angry words from the downstairs corridor came back to her: *I did this without your support or your money, and I'm going to finish it the same way.*

She'd thought he was just driven to do well for his family, but it went deeper than that.

Even metaphorical scars could burn your chest.

* * *

The good thing about watching someone else perform surgery from the gallery? Being able to leave whenever the urge struck. And after it was done, no lumpy mattresses in the on-call room that always smelled a little like feet no matter how frequently staff changed the bedding.

That had been part of the reasoning Kimberlyn had spent the remaining hours in the surgery convincing herself that she shouldn't drag Enzo to the on-call room to violate some rules. At least during those times when she hadn't successfully thrown cold water on her own mood with too many deep thoughts.

Now that they'd reached his car, now that he was driving her home, her list of reasons not to act on that desire shriveled. Kimberlyn paused with her hand on the passenger door handle.

She could take the subway home. That would immediately remove her from temptation. Then, maybe after she got some sleep, she'd feel…remotely sensible about anything pertaining to the man. The subway would allow her to put a damper on things before they got out of control.

And sounded like a terrible idea.

They'd controlled the lust three times now, but the first time he'd immediately left and she had gone to bed. Today's doubleheader left her feeling needy in a way that wasn't even simply about desire. That made it more dangerous to spend twenty minutes in his car, submersed in a cloud of his manly citrusy scent and the memory of firm heat still tingling in her side from having sat tucked against him for hours. Impossible to do and keep her sanity intact.

While she'd stood undecided at his car door, Enzo had gotten in. He leaned over now to catch her eye and asked, "Do you want to stay?" His words, while muffled by the raised window, were still understandable.

She shook her head, then shrugged and sighed.

He rolled down the window, the motion asking her for words.

"I'm just wondering if it's smart to keep hanging out, or whatever it is we're doing." The words rolled out, and she couldn't have said whether she wanted him to talk her out of it or not.

Enzo thought a moment and straightened. The hand resting on his knee moved up toward the ignition. Her stomach bottomed out and she snatched her hand back from the door. He was going to just go? Leave her standing? That would certainly send a message about how much he wanted her. Maybe earlier really had just been about feeling better in the moment…

He plucked the keys from the ignition before she reached panic stage. With one fluid motion he hefted himself from the car. Wherever he wanted to go, whatever he wanted to do, she was going. Even if he didn't say it, she was going to. She couldn't keep treading water around him.

A quick stride brought him around the car and he leaned against her door before speaking. "It's not smart at all."

Maybe he intended to talk her out of it? The look in his eyes was caught somewhere between a lusty smolder and a dare. A look she couldn't pull off if she tried.

He caught one of her hands and tugged until she'd taken the two steps separating them, and found herself chest to chest with him, heart rate soaring. "But I still want to do it. Whatever we're doing."

And more. He definitely wanted more. Thank goodness.

"How bad an idea do you think it is?" Why was she asking him questions? What could he say that would relieve the worry that wasn't going to stand in her way anyway?

What would it do to their relationship? How could he know?

How much would it screw up all their plans?

Could she do one night and return to the trenches the next day?

Had she even been in the freaking trenches yet?

"I need to rate it?" He asked his own question, breaking through the mental wall of flying questions, that flirty demeanor coming back over him, along with a lopsided little-boy grin so at odds with his hands sliding around her waist and down. Soon large hands cupped her rear and squeezed her so close she could feel the jut of his hip bones. So close she imagined she could even feel that delicious V of firm muscle leading down to the heat and firmness she knew she wasn't imagining.

How would he feel? What kind of lover would Enzo be?

Realizing she'd started breathing faster through her mouth, she closed her lips and tried to focus on what he was saying.

"Okay, let me think. On a scale of one to ten, with one being...ice cream for breakfast and ten being...getting hammered before you go to your first chain-saw juggling lesson, it's probably...somewhere in the middle."

A cute smirk followed that completely noncommittal answer.

She had to grin at the flirty fool, both for his examples of bad choices and for sharing her inability to nail down how bad the idea was. "Six?"

He shrugged, and rather than say anything else his hands lifted to her waist, then in one fluid movement dived down below the waistband of her scrubs and the thin cotton panties beneath.

Kimberlyn's breathing stuttered. It had been a long time since she'd been with a man. Before her accident. Well before. So far before that she was having a hard time thinking.

Hot, firm hands squeezing her bare cheeks would've been enough to set her brain to tilt, but Enzo didn't do anything in half measures. His hands slid and gripped, cupping and exploring the flesh.

When he tilted his head, hers fell back, so mad to kiss him that when he stopped with his lips barely brushing hers to whisper, "No scars here," she grabbed his head and kissed him before his words processed, then giggled into his kiss.

Playful. That's what kind of lover Enzo would be. And that was perfect. Playful sex would probably be easier to bounce back from than deep, soul-wrenching sex.

After another few kisses he lifted his head and smiled at her. "Do you really want me to put a number on it?"

Kimberlyn shook her head.

Long fingers tucked around the bottom curve of each cheek, stretching beneath until he had as much sensitive flesh in his hands as he could get, then he squeezed while tilting his head to kiss the side of her neck. Even if she'd demanded a number, that would've effectively shut her up.

Deep in the dark levels of the hospital's parking structure no one would happen upon them. She could probably tear his clothes off right here on the hood and...

Before her intentions crystalized, he slid his hands free from the baggy material, leaving her skin cold, and the rest of her way too aware of the damp garage.

He pivoted her to the side, opened the door and maneuvered her into the opening. "Get in. I demand privacy and somewhere I can take my time. But don't lose that thought."

"Not a chance." She smiled to cover the excited tremble that she was certain he'd see with one look, and did as instructed. Sit. Seat belt. Wait. Don't think about how deliciously aware she was of her body at that second.

In minutes they were out of the parking structure and on the street, heading for the Brooklyn-Battery tunnel.

She couldn't reverse completely, but her sex drive needed to downshift at least a little. And something about their earlier exchange hung around—Enzo avoided. That's how he was going to get through this, by not thinking ahead of time about what the consequences might be. Or maybe he just didn't foresee consequences.

"I have to ask you a question."

"Is it a sexy question?" he asked, and she didn't need to look at him to hear the grin in his voice.

"Not really. I'm just curious about something. You don't seem like the kind of guy who avoids tough subjects, but you kind of do," she said as they entered the tunnel. Dark underground places seemed like the right venue for talking about the subject they'd been circling for weeks: out-of-control attraction and what letting it run wild would mean to them when push came to shove. Or Ootaka began to really push...

"No, I don't. Not without an objective."

"Doesn't everyone who avoids tough subjects do so with an objective? Like the goal of not being scared, worried, sad...or some other unpleasant emotion?"

"Probably."

How was she supposed to react to that? He was good at answering questions in a way that still left her confounded.

"So, by avoiding the subject of how bad an idea it is for us to continue...growing closer, your objective is...?"

"You want to know my intentions, Country Mouse?"

That nickname. Most people who found her name objectionably long called her Cricket, a holdover from a childhood nickname. But somehow, when those words tumbled past his lips, they sounded like an endearment, not like the city slicker making fun of the bumpkin.

"Yes. I want to know your intentions." As all country mice should.

"I intend to take you somewhere private, deprive you of your clothes and ply you with wine and good food until you let me have dessert. I don't even care where. Your place. My place. A motel with a heart-shaped bed and magic fingers. I don't care. It just needs food, a bed and maybe a hot, steamy shower."

The blatant statement gave her another rush of good tingles in all the right places.

She wanted exactly that. "My place. I don't want to go to a skeevy motel."

"Good choice."

Yes, it was. Good choice because she was going to ignore logic. It was a choice that would mean staying with him longer, sharing something that would give them both peace, for a little while at least. She'd just have to take a page out of his book and not question the future for once.

After their long hard day they deserved some good. Something to counter today's heartache. Some way to stop thinking about Mr. Elliot's accident. Stop comparing his accident to hers. Stop wondering if it would have been better for him and his family if she'd failed to recognize the symptoms that had saved him and thus forced them into making such a hard choice after the seemingly good news of his survival.

Stop wondering whether, if the paramedics had made that decision at her accident, Janie would have been the one to survive instead of her.

Kimberlyn fumbled with the door handle as soon as Enzo threw the car into Park. By the time she got out he'd climbed out, shut the door and bounded around to her side. After an obligatory beep to lock the vehicle he grabbed her ponytail in the back, holding her steady as he swooped in and pressed her against the car.

She'd been thinking about kissing him for the past twenty-seven minutes, no matter what else she tried to think about. One more minute until they got inside was entirely too long to wait.

Her heart paused and then galloped hard. His soft lips and demanding tongue, the scrape of the three-day beard he wore like a three-piece suit. Heat, sweetness and need.

The long day had left her raw and hollow, despite the show she put on for him and anyone who looked her way. His hand left her hair and skimmed her body, around her waist to dive into the back of her scrubs.

Someone whistled. Outside. Still outside. "Inside," she panted against his lips, and he nodded, pulling his hands free and turning her in one motion. He walked behind her, propelling her up the stairs with his body.

His breath hot on her neck made her spine curl, and she bumped her rear end ever so slightly against him before she managed to straighten up and not fall.

Falling wouldn't be sexy. At least, not falling outside on the stairs.

She'd never been so thankful for her neurotic tendency to plan for everything—she'd gotten her keys out while still in the car. Now she just had to get the damned thing in the slot.

The end jabbed the dead bolt and slid off to nick the wood.

"Shoot."

He nosed her ear, purring the words so that the baby-fine hairs on the back of her neck stood at attention. "Don't worry, I've got much better aim than that."

He didn't take her keys but he took control of her hand and glided the key into the lock. God help her, he was making unlocking the door sexy, and she was aroused to the point that she was just happy to be more or less in control of her balance.

When it was seated, his hand left to stroke down her body to the heat between her legs. Through the fabric, his strong hands stroked along the seam, those deft fingers pressing firmly to mold the damp material to her.

Sandwiched between him and the door, she managed to click the lock and turn the knob. They staggered through the door. She dropped her bag to free her hands. The door closed somehow, and in three wide strides he'd propelled her backward to the stairs.

"No one here." He leaned back and ripped his shirt off and dropped it on the floor.

The man was fit, lean muscle and definition, short black

hair dusting the olive skin and trailing down over his belly, a path she let her fingertips travel, tracing every dip and swell of the hard muscle beneath.

He knew she had scars, but the filter he'd seen them through before had been clinical, curious. The sexy filter was a lot different, as was seeing them all together rather than one at a time. From the front, she was riddled with scars. When her shirts came off, what would he think? Would he be disappointed? Men were visual creatures...

Thoughts she'd never let herself consider before because of her five-year plan. It didn't include men. Before her accident she'd never considered whether she could please her partner. It annoyed even her that she oscillated between being plagued by guilt or plagued by insecurities.

He leaned back in, arms sliding into the triangle made by the stair at her back, his lips and tongue at the hollow beneath her ear when his hot breath would've been enough to have her arching against him.

She had to say something before her clothes came off and he was confronted with the ugly truth. Seeing it in his eyes might add more emotional scars than she could abide. "Enzo...you're beautiful. I don't have a pretty body anymore..."

He leaned back enough to look at her, his brows pinching in that brooding fashion before he shook his head. "Shut up, Mouse. You're smarter than that."

As soon as the words were out he moved against her, the hard ridge of his barely concealed erection grinding with enough strength to massage the rapidly swelling nub between her legs.

Okay. Point made.

"Not here... Upstairs," she panted, her words breaking over a single spasm of pleasure. Not an orgasm but close already, and if that was any indication...

His answer was another deep, drugging kiss. With every plunge of his tongue he rocked his hips against her.

When another of those prophetic spasms hit her, she cried out blindly.

Enzo could have stayed on the stairs. Hell, he could have stayed outside with her, or in the garage, or in his car pulled to the side of the road.

Anyone else and he might have. But Kimberlyn deserved better. Even if she hadn't been worried about her scars, the idea of someone else catching a glimpse of them together... more like the idea of someone seeing her body...set his teeth on edge. He didn't even want anyone hearing those special cries of pleasure that belonged to him.

And by the sound of things she had already neared orgasm.

Anchoring one arm around her waist, he rose and lifted her with him. "Up."

Her legs didn't want to carry her. She wobbled and grabbed his shoulders and the railing in equal measure, the wild heat in her eyes making the stairs and hallway seem like a thousand-mile journey. They'd never make it like this, and he didn't want her to calm down enough to make it on her own. He wanted her wild-eyed and panting, wanted to be the man who could knock her legs out from under her with her clothes still on.

Knocking her legs out from under her would get them upstairs faster. Bending, he anchored his arm around the backs of her knees so she fell forward over his bare shoulder, and he was off.

"Enzo?"

"Faster." He took the stairs at a jog.

When he reached her unit—another door to get through—he set her down and she handed him the keys, not even attempting to steady her hands enough to get the key in this time.

He kept her in front of him, her back to his front, the sweet curve of that soft little rump almost wrecking his coordination. She waited for him to click the lock, then turned the knob to push into the room.

He looked around enough to orient himself in the low evening light. Clean but the bed unmade, reminding him of how many hours ago they'd been called out of bed to the surgery. His bed remained unmade, too...

"Caren likes pink stuff," she said, curling her fingers in the waistband of his scrubs and pulling him to her from the front now, misinterpreting his expression.

"I like pink stuff, too," he said, unable to keep the little tease in. The door closed with more force than he'd meant to close it. But it was closed.

He reached for the hem of her scrub top and pulled it and the Spandex undershirt off in one motion.

The scar on her chest pulled his gaze, bringing a worry with it. "You've been cleared for sex, right?"

"I'm cleared for normal activity," she mumbled, flipping open the clasp at the back and pulling off the simple white bra and tossing it to the floor. Having her breasts free for inspection and adoration took his attention from the scar... which was just want he'd wanted.

Wrapping one arm around her waist, he kept her moving toward the bed.

She was self-conscious about her scars, and he didn't know whether to pay attention to them or ignore them. What would she prefer? There was plenty to keep his attention without those physical reminders of what she'd been through.

He lay between her legs, her soft breasts mashing against his chest. He wanted to feel the length of her against him, but her legs had wrapped around him and that felt amazing. Until a sneaker hit him in the back, breaking the kiss.

"Sorry." She toed the other one loose and kicked it away from them.

"Don't be sorry. I want you naked, too."

Shoes wouldn't slow them down. He undressed her in

another quick, smooth rush of fabric and then stood back to look at her.

No tan lines. She was naturally tan, and she no longer went out in public in a bathing suit. That shouldn't bother him, but it did.

It didn't make him want her less, but…questions. About her accident, and how she'd been since then. Questions he had no business asking. Willful ignorance could only help him right now. The more he knew, the more he wanted to know. The more he cared. The more confused everything got.

The scent of her skin, the way she arched and moaned when he took one of her nipples into his mouth. That was enough to know for now.

By the time a condom had been secured and rolled on, he was hard to the point of pain.

Go slow. He should go slow. Who knew when she'd last had a lover…?

He stroked the swollen head of his shaft through the slick folds and pushed into her.

Her body opened, wrapping him in heat and clenching hard enough to send shivers racing over his body.

He had to move.

Light-headed and panting, he withdrew and thrust, reveling in every gasp he wrung out of her, in every involuntary twitch of her body, in the way her toes curled against his thighs.

Every second in her was a struggle not to come, and when her eyes screwed shut, blocking him out, that struggle got easier.

And much less satisfying. He wanted to see the unfocused dreamy wonder in her eyes. "Look at me."

Even if his endurance couldn't hold out, he needed the connection. No, he wanted it. It wasn't need. He wanted the connection. He wanted in. Not just inside her soft body, but her—the intimacy that let him feel her pleasure, too. How much he pleased her.

She teetered on the edge, hit-and-run spasms crashing over her like miniature orgasms and threatening his sanity.

When the big one hit and that hot little core began to pulse, his heart thundered in his chest and he trembled from head to toe.

The first wave of climax hit like a thunderclap, stronger than anything he'd ever felt, breaking his rhythm. He'd swear he'd heard it...

One of them cried out.

Her legs clamped around his hips, pulling him into her again, urging him to move, each jerky thrust of his hips rewarded with another shock of pleasure—one he saw reflected in her dazed eyes. A look that no doubt mirrored his own.

When the storm passed, he flung himself onto his back, gulping down air like a drowning man.

She rolled to him and climbed back atop him, tucking her nose under his jaw and whispering, "Hug me. Hug me hard like you did."

When had he hugged her hard? He swallowed, mouth dry, but he couldn't do anything but what she asked. Both arms slipped over her back, squeezing her tight so she'd know he held her.

Her trembling eased as he squeezed her, but his insides still quaked like gelatin.

Grabbing the blanket at his side, he pulled it over them and closed his eyes.

He'd think later. The only thing clear to him right now was that his plans had changed.

He didn't want to think about how.

Kimberlyn awoke hours later, blankets and pillows scattered everywhere, still warm despite only the sheet remaining. Sometime in the hours since they'd fallen asleep they'd rolled. Enzo's big body now nestled behind her.

Although they'd moved, both his arms stayed wrapped around her—one beneath her head looped to rest his hand on the opposite shoulder, the other flung over her waist. Loose, but still around her. Heat at her back, breath in her hair... She could get used to this. Not that she should, but she really could.

The clock on the bedside table cut through the dark. Two in the morning. Right around the time they'd been called in the night before.

Should she wake him up? It would be sweeter if she went to the kitchen and made sandwiches first. Not usually something she'd do. She'd never been the girlfriend who baked or tended. She'd always had something of her own she'd been immersed in. There had been boyfriends, but she'd never felt compelled to take care of them. Probably unsurprising as her mother and father weren't that sort, either. They seemed to love one another, but it wasn't... consuming.

The word fit on so many levels right now.

Carefully, she lifted the arm draped over her and eased out from under it. Even in the dark she found her robe quickly, threw it on and slipped out of her unit to head for the kitchen.

The shirt he'd lost in the foyer was draped over the banister. She winced. Busted. They certainly hadn't taken the time before heading upstairs, and considering the standard of embroidered names their *thing* was no longer any kind of secret. Made it...what did it make it? In not talking about possibilities, they hadn't talked about whether or not they wanted others finding out.

No signs of life in the house. She made the sandwiches, grabbed some water and went back up with his shirt over one shoulder.

The light under her door was on. Enzo had awakened.

She slipped in and found him tying his shoes, dressed except for the top she carried. "Hungry still?" She showed him the plate.

"Yes, but I figured I'd head home and sleep a couple more hours before my shift in the morning." He rose and stepped over, taking his shirt off her shoulder.

Was it walk-of-shame time? She'd been worried about the consequences, but she'd thought they'd be more about work. And happen at work. Not that he'd take off as soon as he woke up.

She must have looked pitiful, because he looked down at the plate. His shirt back on, he gestured. "But I can stick around for a sandwich first."

Definitely crossed the line into Patheticville. This was what regret looked like. Enzo was unhappy they'd ended up here, even if he'd been so certain about everything earlier.

She sat on the edge of the bed and placed the plate to her side. He sat so it was between them, took the water bottle and started eating.

"If I hadn't come back so fast, would you have gone without telling me?"

"No," he answered quickly and then, as if to convince her this was just business as usual, added, "this is none of my business, but when was the last time you were with someone?"

Ah, the reason he'd been eager before and was less eager now. It hadn't lived up to his expectations. Or she hadn't.

The growling in her stomach faded, the sandwich no longer looked good. Maybe after she got this over with, after he'd gone, she could eat it.

"It was before my accident." Tell the truth. Get it over with. "I know it was fast. I'm sure it was…not as fun for you as it could have been. Sorry." Her gaze fell to her lap and a sigh slid out.

"Hey."

He wanted her to look at him, not something she was

keen to do. The only thing faster than his exit was how awkward the aftermath was becoming.

Just smile through it. Let him off the hook.

She straightened, her lips curling up slightly at the corners, she imagined. Or maybe they were just a straight line. Anything was better than turned down or wobbling.

"It's okay. I know this wasn't something that could ever happen again anyway. And it probably wouldn't have if yesterday hadn't been so difficult for both of us." She stood up and tightened the belt on her robe, willing it to be longer. Why had she gotten the short robe? Robes were supposed to be concealing and warm, not with a bouncy hemline for spring. Stupid.

"You didn't disappoint me. I just was thinking about how things were at the hospital, and that it could be messy. For us. Could upset plans, and neither of us wants that."

She forced herself to make eye contact with him, even though she wanted to shove him out the door, then maybe have a lobotomy or find someone to wash her brain. "You're right. We'll go back to business as usual. It's not a big deal."

It was a big deal if someone like Enzo could see past her scars and all her stupid issues. Which he had, she thought.

And none of that was the right reaction to have. A relationship wasn't in her plan. No men. The plan said no relationships. A one-night stand? Well, that could make it through on a technicality. But, still, he could have made it a whole night. This was more like a half-night stand.

She was still fuzzy from days of sleep deprivation. Not her best thinking state. At least not when emotions got into the mix.

"I need sleep," she said, to start him moving again. "I'm on the afternoon shift tomorrow, so I'm going to inhale the sandwich and get back to sleep. The door downstairs will lock when you close it. It always requires a key to come in."

He nodded, picking up the other half of his sandwich in one hand and his keys in the other.

His gaze tracked to the bed behind her, and for a second it felt as if he might stay. As if he might just say to the devil with all the things that had been said and stay.

"I'm on the morning shift," he said instead, the words shutting down her train of thought. It was just as well. She'd have let him stay for sure...because of pride? What was that?

Enzo stood there a moment, watching the angry tilt of her chin and the way her arms crossed and her brow furrowed. He could make her smile if he stayed. Go back to bed. Not sleep... Let things get messier than they'd already gotten.

He didn't even know at what point the line had been crossed, but it had been. For both of them. It hadn't just been sex. It hadn't just been comfort or need. She'd felt something. He knew she had. And he'd known it when she'd rolled with him. It had been in the hug she'd begged for. That hadn't been about desire. It had been something much deeper, something she thought he could give her.

Not daring to kiss her goodbye, Enzo nodded and stepped toward the door. As soon as it swung shut, he heard the lock.

Message received: unwelcome.

Good. He should be.

CHAPTER TEN

ENZO FOUND KIMBERLYN in the locker room, staring at the posting Ootaka had made earlier. It had been six whole days since he'd slunk out of her bedroom. Six days of not speaking. Six days of barely making eye contact. It had felt like six months of Herculean effort to pull it off. It felt almost as hard to approach her now...

That morning Ootaka had posted an announcement that the deadline for application to his fellowship had been moved up. Rather than them having until January, he was going to post his decision in three weeks.

Three weeks could be a really long time—but under a time crunch, time perception changed.

"Hey," he said behind her, since he'd managed to walk up without her noticing again. The woman was disturbingly easy to sneak up on. Anytime she was alone she was often so absorbed in her own thoughts that everything else went on without her.

And right now he knew what those thoughts were. For a fleeting few seconds he was glad that the deadline had been moved. At least now she didn't have to think about the ways he'd disappointed her.

"You okay?"

Because, of course, that wasn't a stupid thing to ask.

Kimberlyn turned to him and shrugged, not making eye contact again. "Do you really want to know?"

The same question he'd asked her before, the same question he asked himself all the time.

"I want to know."

Shaking her head, she moved on. "Do we know why he's moving it up?"

Still not looking at him—and not answering his question—she sat on the bench and studied her fingernails, picking at them as if there was a speck of something she just couldn't get rid of trapped beneath the carefully tended manicure.

"He has to go to Japan. Someone in his family is ill. When you have one the world's best surgeons sharing your gene pool, if something goes wrong you get to call in favors," Enzo said, tension eating at his shoulders again.

"And he'll be gone a long time, I guess."

"He might be." Still trying to relax, he sat on the bench beside her. His knee touched hers and he slid a couple of inches back. Too close. No touching. "He doesn't like to leave things unfinished."

She nodded, her brows as pinched as her lips were pursed.

Unlike Ootaka, he'd left whatever was between him and Kimberlyn unfinished. But this time his avoidance wasn't because he didn't want to know anything that might change his plans. Because he had no plans for once in his life. He didn't know what to do. One of them was going to be disappointed soon, and the way things were going with her...

"There's not a lot of time left for you to catch up." He didn't quite know how to phrase it so that it wasn't offensive. Being blunt was so much easier, but somewhere along the way he'd started using the same temperance with Kimberlyn as he did with his family. He didn't do that with any other colleagues, or even friends in the hospital. He certainly didn't do that with Sam, and Sam was a good friend.

"It's not, but I can still do it. I've always responded well to a ticking clock."

"Not me." His hand itched to touch her. She was right there, and no one else was in the locker room to disrupt them. "I tend to become a—"

"Hyper-focused jerk?"

"That," he agreed, trying and failing to smile.

"So are you here to warn me or am I still not competition?"

"No." But this was why he shouldn't have asked. "I think you're more competition than anyone else in the program."

Competition enough to make him feel awful. She'd definitely have the spot if he weren't around.

"That's something, I guess."

"I want to know about your heart now." The words had come out before he had even consciously thought about them. Had just appeared in his head and dashed out before he could consider the ramifications of asking right now.

"You mean my surgery?"

He definitely didn't want to know any more details. But he still asked, "Why was your chest cracked?"

"Aortic dissection."

What Elliot had suffered.

"Did it show with tamponade? Did they catch it during your bowel resection?" Please say yes. Make it as uneventful as possible.

She shook her head. "No, I didn't have the tamponade. The tear was small, and the blood wasn't leaking much into the chest cavity at that point."

"How did they find it?" Why was he even asking this? It was in the past. He couldn't fix her past. He couldn't fix anything for her.

"I went into shock in the ICU," she murmured. "But Dr. Anderson got me into an OR just in time."

His stomach churned just knowing how close she'd come to death. How close he'd come to losing her or never having known her. "You've come back from a lot." Maybe she could pull this off in the eleventh hour.

"I'm trying."

He watched her. She answered his questions. She wasn't yelling at him for the worst after-sex exit in history. It'd be better if she did. It'd be better than talking about this stuff. And people said talking helped problems... "You're succeeding," he argued, at a loss for anything else to say.

"Not as well as I'd like," she murmured, standing suddenly to pace around the locker room. Any second she'd be gone, maybe even just to get away from him.

"Have you thought about any other programs?" He dug into the pocket of his jacket to fish out his tablet. A couple of ticks and he turned it toward her to read.

She squinted at the tablet and the small colorful image of the whole document, "You have a spreadsheet of other trauma fellowships?"

He nodded. "Listed by desirability and the habits of the board to choose from pools outside their residency program."

Unlike Ootaka, who only chose from those he'd witnessed in the OR.

"So you made that when you were deciding where to request placement?" She crossed her arms as she finally fixed him with that squint that was becoming a scowl.

Her indirect way of asking if he'd done that for her or for him. "No. I did it a few days ago." Because he needed to try to fix things somehow.

And maybe he was working on his guilt after they'd banished a hard, long day by falling into bed together.

"For me," she said.

It wasn't even a question now.

"I care about you, Kimberlyn. I know you're not making a backup plan, and I was going to talk to you about it in a while, but now that Ootaka has moved things up it seemed like the time."

She unfolded her arms long enough for her cool fingers to touch his wrist and push away the hand holding his device. "Gee, thanks. I care about you, too, even though I think you're extremely arrogant and blind in this matter. It's not over just because he announced it will be decided sooner rather than later. I still have time."

"You have time to try." He tapped a couple more times on the tablet, emailing her the spreadsheet, since she refused to look at it now. "But I can't let my standing carry me. The next three weeks you're going to be working to catch up, and I'm going to be working to increase my lead."

"And your point is?"

"My point is that you should at least make a backup plan." Please, just let him fix something.

"Have you applied anywhere else?"

He dropped the tablet back into his pocket. "Not yet."

"But you're going to?"

"I haven't decided." He also hadn't decided until that second that he had to go back to maintaining that distance from her for the next three weeks. Not just avoidance. He... needed to treat her like Lyons. She made him soft.

"I'm not giving up, but I will apply for a few others. Ones I've already decided are my backups. Because I have to go somewhere, and I'm practical enough to know that even if I want this, I should spread my eggs among many baskets." She stood up, a tug of her top straightening her appearance, and headed for the door.

"Where are you going?"

A short laugh and she called as she kept walking, "To start crafting my plan for world domination."

"Wait." He caught up in a few strides and grabbed her elbow to stop her sassy exit. "I need to say something else."

She groaned. "You're in a hole, Enzo. Stop digging."

"It's a warning."

"Fine. Warn away." She crossed her arms again and watched him work out what he wanted to say. She'd spent the week regretting the sex, and now it was only worse. She'd been an idiot to think she could do a one-night thing without getting wrapped up in it. No doubt this was what she deserved for getting relaxed with him.

"I said I don't respond well to a ticking clock. I don't." He shrugged, as if he had more to say but didn't know quite how to say it. "Having my plans and my schedules messed with makes me more focused and competitive."

"Warning received—you're going into hyperactive jerk mode, like when you ran ahead to Ootaka."

"Don't take it personally."

"Of course not. You know, if you're going to be nasty or ignore me, like you have been, then just do it all the time. All this flipping back and forth between being a flirty smooth talker and a bastard is giving me motion sickness. If you have a decent bone in your body, or even if you just want to give a nod to fair play, pick a personality and stick with it." She really was getting used to the city if she could have a fight like this and not throw up afterward. "And just so we're clear, whichever personality wins, let him know that there won't be any further naked stuff with me."

Enzo had known this talk wouldn't go well. How could it go well when his instincts were at war? Like the ones that said he should ask her questions constantly at odds with his self-preservation instincts that told him to shut up. He couldn't blame her for thinking of him as a Jekyll and Hyde character.

But that didn't mean he had to like it. His lips firmed and his gaze slid down to her elbow where he'd stopped her flight, where he'd been stroking the skin in a classic comforting maneuver. That instinct to comfort always rose back up, but he was still the kind of man she should be warned about.

She pulled her elbow free and he let her. It was harder to think straight when they touched in any fashion, but especially flesh to flesh. "Good luck, Dr. DellaToro. And don't go complaining to Sam about me, either."

"I wouldn't do that."

"Good. He doesn't want to be in the middle, and he deserves that consideration."

His ears were probably lucky that the door she stormed out of couldn't slam.

Kimberlyn went directly from the locker room to Ootaka's office, where she found him doing paperwork. A short knock announced her and he looked up, motioning her inside.

"Dr. Ootaka, I know your mind must be going a million directions right now, but I need to say a couple of things. First, I'm sorry to hear that your family is having a difficult time. It's the right thing for you to go to them, and everyone understands that the deadline has been moved up."

He nodded, gesturing to her to sit in the chair on the other side of his desk, but went back to writing whatever he'd been working on—some form or another. "You want to ask about your chances with the fellowship, Dr. Davis?"

"No." She sat as invited but didn't relax, keeping her posture as straight and rigid as she'd always been taught to do. Situations like this demanded formality, that she be the proper and polite lady physically, even if her mouth was about to go a different direction than deferential etiquette drilled into her.

"I want to assist you in surgery. I understand your custom is to go slowly and let the other surgeons vet the residents before they are invited into your OR, but I've proven myself already."

She took a breath. Should she bring her personal history into this? It might seem like a request for him to take pity on her when her motivation was entirely the opposite. She wanted to show him she could take charge, prove her spine existed, and telling him everything—or almost everything—would demonstrate that. He didn't need to know more than that she was motivated. "How much do you know about my time and residency at Vanderbilt?"

"I have received a recommendation from Dr. Anderson. He speaks highly of your skill and focus."

She smiled when she heard the surgeon's name spoken, her resolve firming up. "He's had a special view of my focus."

"How so?"

"Dr. Anderson put me back together after a catastrophic car accident six weeks before my fourth year of residency was supposed to start." Her voice hadn't wavered at all. No emotion. She could do this.

That made his pen stop. He lifted his gaze from the paper and gave her his full attention. "I did not know you'd had an accident."

Think about the wreck as if it was one of her patients. Not her. Faking distance was something that had worked moderately for her in the past. "I had an obvious serious bowel injury when they cut me from the car. A piece of metal that had gone through my jejunum. He removed it and repaired my bowel. I also had a broken femur and torn rotator cuff. The structural orthopedic repairs that take a backseat to the life-threatening ones. While I was in ICU after the bowel repair I crashed. He had to crack my chest. I had a small aortic dissection that was taking its time bleeding out."

She took a deep breath. She should have stopped using *I this, I that*. She really needed to work on a narrative that could give her distance. Talking about the accident always left her feeling bare.

"How far behind your classmates are you?"

"Just one year," she answered, then drew a deep breath. "I'm not telling you this because I want you to think that I'm in need of special consideration. I just want you to see how hard I can fight for something that I want, and how motivated I am not just to succeed but to succeed spectacularly. I deferred my residency for a year to heal and work through the physical therapy necessary to come back from that. Vanderbilt let me defer that a year—it was my school and the hospital where I spent so much time recovering.

"But in all the time I spoke with Dr. Anderson in those first weeks I understood that sometimes fate interacts with our lives and changes the course forever. I know that I survived because of one of your fellows. And I know that I want to be that doctor for others. Give me another chance in your OR to prove myself."

Her knee started to bounce. She stopped it. She'd gotten through all that with a strong voice, clean...mostly free of emotion. Not the time to blow it now. Thinking about the emotions crossing Ootaka's face, as subtle as they were, could blow it for her. He had the kind of poker face that would clean up in Vegas.

"The next surgery is yours, Dr. Davis," he finally said.

She hadn't expected him to make a decision now. She'd expected that he would say that he'd heard her and that he would bear her request in mind—something that deflected from having to commit to a course of action. But he really didn't deflect.

She should've listened to Enzo on that one if nothing else—he didn't like to leave decisions hanging.

"Th-thank you," she managed, though a small stammer at the start probably gave away some kind of emotion. Was surprise a bad emotion to display?

"I had already intended to invite the top trauma residents into surgery in the coming weeks as a testing ground, but I appreciate your directness. I expect no less than that on the floor."

Nodding, she stood and offered her hand to him, repeating again, because she just didn't know what else to say, "Thank you."

It had been a brisk pace to learn the difference between the attitudes of the two different hospitals, but she was finally getting it. And there was something to be said for the direct route. While it didn't aim to spare the feelings of anyone, it also didn't build false hope. The cuts were quick and clean, and she could appreciate that.

When he'd shaken her hand, she headed out. He didn't comment on her accident, and she was thankful for that. As good a face as she'd just put on for him, it was faltering.

Once in the safety of the hallway, she scrambled to the nearest stairwell for a moment of solitude. She just needed to catch her breath, let her hands steady and her heart slow down before it started to feel as if it was doing somersaults.

Her heart, like the rest of her, would have to get used to the new normal eventually. Probably sometime after the blunt, quick-cut method of dealing with others came a little more naturally to her.

Though it kind of felt as if she'd already done that with Enzo back in the locker room.

In the lead-up to Ootaka leaving, the older surgeon had decided that the best way to test his top two candidates was to pair them off in surgeries where one led and the other assisted, then switch it around for the next surgery.

Starting tonight, Enzo and Kimberlyn were both on the evening shift with Ootaka so that they could be around for the busiest times for trauma surgeons. Enzo had never had a shift where something interesting didn't happen, but his hairiest nights were always on the weekend. Friday could be counted on to bring the hairy.

Since their quarrel about backup plans, something had gone down between Kimberlyn and Ootaka, resulting in her being his primary assistant for the past eleven days. And he was going to hold the line and not ask her any questions even if it killed him. Now, if he could just stop thinking about things…and her.

His phone buzzed. Text from Ootaka.

Time to work.

Enzo hit the door of the on-call room at a jog and headed for the OR he'd been summoned to.

He would be the first one to lead surgery. He'd been around longest, he'd had the most time with Ootaka in the OR and it probably said something about how much Ootaka trusted him that he gave him first crack.

It didn't do much to improve his mood.

Kimberlyn was at one of the sink bays, scrubbing in, when he arrived. "Bashing trauma," she said to him as soon as he entered.

He tied on his cap as he stepped to the second sink bay. She'd have to talk to him for the surgery. And the other way around. "From what?"

"Fight in Central Park." She shook her head. "He's young, Enzo."

Fight? Young? If it was a kid... "How old?"

"Fourteen."

His dinner felt like lead in his stomach. Not a little kid but young enough. He'd seen his fair share of fights in his neighborhood, but now that he knew exactly how much damage a fist could do to internal organs, the violence he'd grown up around and accepted as a matter of course sickened him.

That insensitivity to violence was part of the cultural divide he'd always been aware of with his father's departure from their lives—so aware of it that by the time he'd become a teenager he'd gotten into fights to reinforce that difference. Yelling at him as he had over the transplant was just a step away from throwing punches, but a step he'd learned not to take if he could avoid it.

"You okay?" she asked, the first personal thing she'd said to him since he'd bailed on her while inhaling a sandwich.

"I hate violence. Medical school ruined boxing for me. Ruined a lot of my enjoyment with sports of all kinds, but violence is especially disturbing. People think that if there isn't a weapon involved, nothing too bad can happen."

"Tree limb," she said, throwing him briefly. "That was

the weapon. Over by the carousel, they said. I don't know where that is, but..."

"You haven't been to Central Park since you've been here?" He asked the question as if he didn't know how busy she'd been, even before she'd become Ootaka's new toy. The reading and the studying could be done in Central Park, but maybe not if you were new to the city.

"No. But I went to the Statue of Liberty and the Empire State Building."

Enzo groaned. "I thought you'd flock to the green places, Country Mouse."

Damn, he shouldn't have called her that.

The tiny smile she gave him cracked him in the chest. He'd missed her.

Professional distance and avoiding anything else couldn't continue. He had to come up with some way to make things work out well for her, even after the fellowship was announced. He'd give his left kidney if Ootaka would just take them both on...

When they exited to the OR, nurses met them, gloved and gowned them. Ootaka had already scrubbed in and was in the OR, waiting for them both.

No instruction, but he took a position beside Enzo and waited, watching.

Enzo didn't even need to palpate the abdomen. He could see distinct swelling in the right quadrant of the boy's belly. Liver damage. And the only way to verify if it was bleeding, shattered or merely bruised and swollen was with visual inspection.

"Number twenty-two scalpel," he announced and made a diagonal incision below the lower curve of the last rib.

Kimberlyn was there immediately with retractors, helping to open the boy's belly so that he could get eyes on it. They could do this much together, at least.

"Narrate, Doctor," Ootaka instructed.

"Lots of blood," Enzo announced, and Kimberlyn was

there with pads to help absorb the blood. "Coming from the liver." He examined more closely and announced, "The organ has opened in two fissures."

"Action?" Ootaka prompted.

"Trim it and assure blood supply," Enzo answered.

Standing across from her now, while better than total avoidance, still wasn't enough. He wanted her in his life. The whole situation would be so much easier if he could just point to their relationship fissures, trim off the damaged parts, make sure the rest was fed… Was that possible? Was that how people healed damaged relationships?

Kimberlyn swapped the saturated pads with fresh ones as Enzo worked, working to not only anticipate his needs but also to keep her hands out of the way. Every now and then she felt his eyes on her over their patient. Not lingering, just a glance she was so aware of it might as well be a touch.

The rest of the team worked on the periphery, mostly silent like Ootaka, but it felt like just the two of them. She should be managing the team, too, not replaying him calling her Mouse again. The warmth in his voice and that rascally way he flirted always muddied up her thinking.

Like now. Manage the team. She checked vitals, blood, and had one of the techs reposition the light so that it lit up the body cavity better.

"I'd like to give him blood, Dr. DellaToro," she announced, because that lesson would never leave her. As he worked on trimming away the shattered parts of the boy's liver, she swapped the pads again, still trying to control the bleeding. "He needs clotting factors."

"Agreed." Enzo looked at the monitors to get a reading on the blood pressure, which was much lower than he wanted it to be.

Normally, in the case of extreme abdominal trauma, they went in multiple times to make repairs with periods to stabilize in between. First, stop blood loss. Close lightly.

Wait. Go in again after the patient had been stabilized to avoid shock, do the real repairs. But the nature of this boy's wounds made it harder to do a hit-and-run. He'd keep bleeding if they didn't get the damaged tissue out.

When Enzo had gotten the liver whittled down and in better shape, Kimberlyn pulled out the last round of cloths after they'd applied coagulants and frowned at the fluid on the pads. "Doctor...we're missing something."

Attention pulled from the cavity, Enzo tilted his head to get a better look at the pads and saw it—something there besides blood. "Is that bile? Damned tree limb," he muttered and immediately regretted it. Emotion. Ootaka. But he didn't dwell on it.

"I think it's from the stomach..." She didn't sound as sure as she had been sounding, but it was the time to sound uncertain if you were uncertain. They both gently moved tissues to the side to trace the leak.

Ootaka said nothing yet.

Enzo was about to ask his opinion, mentally sorting through the solid and hollow organs that could be leaking...

Wasn't the stomach.

Not the kidneys.

Not the intestines...

"Pancreas." He moved the stomach aside to visualize the pancreas.

Kimberlyn hurried to get irrigation and suction tools. "If the pancreas is leaking..."

"We can't close."

The only thing the pancreas leaked was digestive fluids. If they closed him up and waited for him to stabilize, everything in the vicinity would be damaged just like food broken down in digestion by those same fluids.

Sometimes what you didn't want to know could kill you. Or at least cause a lot of damage.

They found the damaged section and trimmed it in much

the same fashion as they had the liver. "Good eye, Dr. Davis."

They worked together, and that felt good, too.

When the pancreas had been drained and repaired, they put a mesh in place and stitched the skin closed as they'd likely have to open him up again later.

Ootaka said very little during the whole surgery. Enzo would have liked to pretend that was a good sign, but he would've probably only spoken up if they'd been going down the wrong path. Their performance could have been simply adequate and he'd respond the same.

She'd been the first to spot trouble with this shared patient, too. Seemed like the kind of thing that would usually bother him. But for some reason it didn't. He'd have to think about that sometime. Later.

CHAPTER ELEVEN

A KNOCKING ON her door crept into Kimberlyn's dream.

Then a voice calling.

A man.

Sam.

Behind his loud summons dragging her from sleep, she heard a smaller sound. Tiny, in fact. Had Sam gotten a kitten?

Kimberlyn dragged her still fully clothed self out of the bed and shuffled to the door.

Long shift. Long week. Long year... Or six. Or ten... Long surgery—or series of surgeries on the one patient. Gunshot. She'd call it a gut shot but the bullet had bounced around in there so much that the track hadn't been confined to the gut.

Enzo had assisted, and it had gone well... He hadn't made her look bad—not that she thought he would anymore. There had been a point where they had both been in need of instruction, and Ootaka had stepped in, but whatever the surgeon had been hoping his plan would evoke in them had failed to happen.

"I'm coming," she grumbled, hoping to stop the knocking before her head exploded.

One of her shoes was still on, but the other? Missing. Her lopsided stride made the soreness in her overworked and abused body that much more pronounced.

Too sleepy to try to manage her balance while kicking off the other shoe, she just went with it.

Tomorrow afternoon Ootaka had scheduled the announcement of his newly selected fellow for the following two years.

One of her eyes was also not working properly. Out of focus, no doubt from the makeup she'd failed to take off... however long ago she'd collapsed into bed.

Could you get a hangover from not sleeping?

Two misses of the lock and knob later, she managed to crack the door open and glare with her one good eye at Sam.

The Scot had a baby. Not a baby kitten. A baby human.

A baby human she knew!

Instantly much more awake, she swung the door open and reached out to take one of Maya's little hands. "You brought Maya to see me?"

Shy, the tiny almost-toddler buried her face in Sam's shoulder.

"Aww, she doesn't remember me."

"It's been a couple of months since that dinner," Sam reminded her, grinning.

Not that she could say anything about sparing adoring looks for the little princess. She hadn't even treated Maya and she already had a big squishy smile in place for her. "She remembers you, though."

"I see her at least every couple of weeks." Sam rubbed Maya's back and then coached her to say something.

Whatever she said, the only thing Kimberlyn thought she might have caught was a "Jo" in there somewhere. But she couldn't swear to it.

Sam placed a fancy cream-colored envelope in Maya's hand and told her to give it to Kimberlyn.

"The world's tiniest and most adorable mail carrier." Kimberlyn took it with extravagant thanks and praise, and

then a somewhat less excited question directed at Sam.
"What is this?"

"I believe it's called extortion," Sam explained, "Or
blackmail. I can't keep them separate."

"Okay if I open my extortion envelope?"

"Yep." Sam rubbed Maya's back again, the little girl
curling back against him. She stole everyone's heart.
"We're going to go. Sophie is waiting downstairs to take
the munchkin home."

She said her goodbyes, closed the door and opened the
envelope.

Inside was an invitation on extremely nice stationery,
written by someone with excellent penmanship. So not
Enzo.

Invitation to Central Park that night. Suggestions about
attire. Directions to which entrance to use into the park.

The right edge of the invitation had been embossed with
tiny gold hoofprints running up the side, and the envelope
had one sticky pink handprint on the corner.

Definitely extortion. Involving Maya and Sam? Pretty
much meant she had to go.

But she pretended she didn't. Because she hadn't yet
gotten over her willful stupidity when it came to that man,
and she fell for the hit-and-run, guerrilla-style romance
tactics every time.

Kimberlyn bypassed the subway in favor of a taxi to take
her to the park. While technically not nighttime yet, it was
close enough that she didn't want to ride the subway. She
might never get used to that.

Her taxi stopped at the gate she'd been directed to, and
Enzo stood waiting for her in something other than scrubs.
She rarely saw him in anything else. His corduroy jacket
was the color of old beaten leather, somehow straddling
the same lines he straddled daily. Uptown tailoring on

casual fabrics. Everything else selected to blend into the background.

"I'm glad you listened to my wardrobe suggestion," Enzo said when he got closer to her, hand outstretched. "I was afraid that you wouldn't even have winter clothing, being from the South."

"I grew up in the Smoky Mountains, I have winter clothes. It snows there and everything." She didn't take his hand. It was a step too far. Even with gloves on. She'd dragged herself to the park to meet him, but she couldn't hold hands with him.

Without missing a beat, he stepped to her side and put his arm around her waist. The man was either 100 percent focused on her or utterly ignoring her. There hadn't been any touching since the sex. Heck, there hadn't any anything outside work since the unfortunate decision to go home together had ended with his late-night scramble to get away.

"Why did you invite me here, Enzo?" She pretended his arm around her didn't feel good.

"You said you hadn't been to Central Park before."

"I haven't." This entrance of the park was actually fairly close to their hospital. She could have come straight there from work any number of days, but she never put sightseeing high on her list of things to do. There was always too much work to do, too many things she needed to read, too much to worry about and keep up with the chores of daily living—feeding herself, having clean clothes, sleep... "But that's not what I meant and you know it. No double-talk tonight, no answering without answers. Why now?"

"Why not?" he answered in that annoying way of his, then nodded to the horse-drawn carriage. The driver of the beautiful white carriage was watching them.

"I'm going to leave if you don't start— Is that carriage for us?" The tirade she was working up to died in her throat as she took in the white carriage with its red velvet lining, and the gorgeous white horse pulling it. "Did you rent us a carriage?"

"I've never been in one, but I heard they're nice."

His hand shifted to the small of her back, steering her toward the carriage. Rather than pushy and demanding, it felt like a hug. Caring. Protective. And she was still a woman… What woman could say no to a carriage ride through Central Park?

"You like to play dirty."

"Not always." He murmured the argument.

If he wasn't playing dirty, then this was him playing nice? Suddenly he'd decided to…

Her feet turned to lead, the tread catching on the sidewalk so she stumbled ever so slightly.

He was trying to soften the blow. Ootaka must have told him already.

The fellowship was his.

His hand shot up under her arm to stop her from falling. "Whoa, you all right?"

"Fine," she said quickly, waving a hand to him and calmly extracting her arm. "I just scuffed the bottom of my shoe. No big deal. But thank you." She forced a laugh and a smile she didn't feel. "I guess I'm having a clumsy day. Good thing we're going to ride through the park. Trusting my feet sounds like a bad idea."

A hop and a couple of quick steps pulled her ahead and she reached the carriage, climbed in and settled into the plush velvet seating without any assistance. All around the rim of the back of the carriage white twinkle lights had been installed. So cheerful and dazzling—something a good sport should be, too.

Whatever else had gone on between them, she'd still be happy for him as soon as it settled in. Giving the question voice right now sounded wrong. And completely out of line with the romantic aura these carriages always carried, especially on a crisp October evening that had finally started to feel like autumn.

Enzo climbed in beside her and then slid her over to tuck against his side.

He probably had to agree to some kind of nondisclosure until Ootaka could make the announcement tomorrow. Tomorrow, when all the things that they'd spent the past months denying would actually evaporate. The romantic carriage ride through the park was just an overture, and one she needed to get past rather than be swept up by. "So, tomorrow Ootaka is making his announcement."

Enzo looked out the side of the carriage as it started rolling and was soon off on the trails down into the park. "Yes, it is. I thought maybe this was the only chance I'd have to bring you to experience some quintessential New York. After tomorrow, one of us might not want to be around the other...probably even more so than the past couple of weeks."

"Maybe," she conceded. But, then, her chances with the fellowship had never been very high. She could let disappointment color the whole evening, or she could enjoy being there with him and not let her issues ruin this for him. "But, for the record, I didn't want to not be around you the past couple weeks, so I'm guessing you mean you didn't want to be around me."

He reached for a lap blanket and shook it out over their laps, uncharacteristically direct when he answered, "I just didn't know how."

"And now you do?

He gave a noncommittal shrug, tucking the blanket around her thigh and then laying his arm around her shoulders again. "Now it doesn't matter anymore. There's nothing either of us can do to change whatever Ootaka is going to decide. He will pick one of us. The other..."

"Will be left trying to pick up the pieces and figure out their new path." She finished that statement, going with the subterfuge. Sometimes it helped to pretend that neither of them knew what they were talking about.

He turned his head and brushed his lips across her temple. "If it's me who gets the fellowship, then I want to help you find another good program, to help somehow. And if it's you—" she didn't need to look at him to hear the strains of a rascally smile threatening "—I want you to baby me as I dramatically mope, brood and wallow in a manly fashion."

A grin tickled the corners of her mouth. Cute. A good time to play along. "Okay. I'll bring you cookies that someone else baked. So they can be edible."

She'd spent the majority of the past couple of weeks wanting to talk to him and wrestling her own willpower. Now that it seemed there was nothing left to do but wait for the official word, maybe they could finally talk. Maybe she could enjoy his company without feeling the ax over her head or that usual guilt eating at her.

"I've spent a lot of time making contingency plans the past month. It's not my usual custom. I don't like to give myself room for other plans, in case it jinxes me. But I had a list of other programs, and I cross-referenced it with the spreadsheet you sent. I thought knowing there were other options would make it easier to wait while feeling like I was being proactive or something. But I'm still antsy and irrevocably behind." And full of dread. Or she had been before she'd realized the race was over—some heady cocktail of excitement and dread.

"Behind?"

"I intended to already be in my fellowship by now. I really shouldn't have even been eligible for Ootaka's."

"You never told me what you wanted to study before your accident."

She'd never told him a lot of things. "I dithered between neuro and cardiothoracic."

"Wanted the exciting, hard ones, eh?"

"I guess." She let herself rest her head back on his shoulder and watched the trees overhead. "But all that changed. I'm not sorry it did. I like feeling like I have a calling... I just don't like how it all came about."

"Speaking with your surgeon?"

She tilted her head to look at him and then focused again on the canopy overhead. The sun was low enough now on the horizon that streaks of pink and purple sky showed through the patches of empty air among the brightly colored autumn leaves. "That's not really what did it. Dr. Anderson did help me, as much as he could, but I started those conversations when he came to see me every day on rounds..."

When Kimberlyn hesitated, Enzo looked at her face again. She wasn't looking at him. Her head was tilted back so that she could look at the trees overhead. Was the hesitation about him or the accident? She'd gotten the stiff-upper-lip thing down to an art. When the moment stretched on he prompted her, "But?"

She shrugged and finally looked at him. The sadness that always lurked in her eyes wasn't disguised at all now. "You ask me about my accident relatively frequently, but you never ask the one question everyone else asks."

There were a lot of questions about her accident that Enzo avoided asking. It was like a big bomb hanging over their heads, where all the wires were red so there was no way to know how to stop it from detonating. No way to fix things. That question—like all emotional questions—felt like adding another wire... But her pointing to that question announced its importance, and he couldn't ignore that. "What question is that?"

"You've never asked if I was alone in the car."

"No?" He thought about the things she'd said to him about the accident. She had snuck a couple of *"we's"* into the telling here and there, but usually it had sounded like a one-person story. And he'd gone with that idea because it was safe, and kept him from feeling that pain with her. "Who was in the car with you?"

"My best friend, Janie McIntyre."

The physical details were so much easier to deal with. He got information, but it was safer. The wreck was physically in the past. He knew what had caused the wreck—shredded tire on the road. He knew that the car had been upside down off a highway bridge but not in the water. He knew when it had happened. He knew the surgeries that it had taken to repair her body. He didn't know how long she'd waited for rescue, if she'd been conscious and scared at the time. He hadn't asked the questions that hurt him to contemplate. He hadn't asked if she had been alone because both answers were terrible in their own way, so he didn't think about it. "Who was driving?"

She looked back to the tree canopy and the sky beyond. "Me."

The finality in her voice pinged like the sudden sour taste in the back of his mouth.

If this conversation had been digging into his old wounds, he'd be looking for an escape hatch right about now. Hearing the pain in her voice, seeing the slight tremble of her lower lip as she looked skyward...hurt. That's why he didn't ask questions. Yes, it was selfish. It was the best way to keep from being eaten by the pain of loved ones.

Which, he suddenly realized, was a tactic he'd learned from his father.

Was that why Lyons...?

Not the time to think about Lyons. Everyone had reasons for the things they did, and right now he didn't care about those reasons. He cared about her. She wanted to tell him something, and she needed help getting it out. He asked the question burning a hole in his gut. "Where's Janie now?"

He watched the delicate column of her throat move as she swallowed and then she whispered the words. "She died."

Of course she had, and he should've known that weeks ago. He had to stop managing his responsibility and moderating his emotional response by minimizing his information about them.

He pulled her a little tighter against him. "At the scene? Were you aware...?"

His voice broke in a decidedly unsexy rasp over the second question. As much as she was forcing herself into other actions than she'd like, so was he. His instincts all told him to stop digging, but digging was precisely what he needed to do. If he didn't need to, he wouldn't have questions. He worried about her all the time anyway. Ignorance hadn't been helping. It had just let him pretend it helped.

"When the EMTs got the car peeled open, I was unconscious, skewered by a long piece of metal, but my vitals were fairly stable. They told me Janie was awake and able to talk and answer their questions. She asked them to take me first. They decided that I had the worst injuries, so they did as she asked. She died while another unit was working on getting her out."

Those feelings he could understand, without much more digging. She'd turned toward trauma because she was seeking balance. She'd been saved by one of Ootaka's fellows, and her friend had died because of her accident.

He pulled her more snugly against him and reached across her lap to catch her closest hand. What could he say? What was he supposed to say?

"That's awful. I'm sorry." The cold autumn air burned his eyes.

She nodded, the dampness in her eyes tearing at him.

With his new resolve Enzo kept her close and kept asking questions.

When it seemed as if she'd finally gotten it out, he pulled a bag from behind them, because doing something helped. "Hold this." Settling it on her lap, he pulled out a thermos and poured into the lid some of that gross mocha coffee she and Tessa were always drinking. Doing something helped. "We'll have to share the cup."

She accepted it with a couple of sips, then offered the cup back to him.

He'd planned to take her to the carousel—they weren't running it yet, that was still a couple weeks away, but when he'd thought to do this, he'd expected it would be a nice, romantic ride...

"What else is in your bag?"

"Stew, funnily. I conned Mom into making us something and she sent me off with two containers of soup and some good bread. There are usually a few vendors operating at this hour in the better lit areas of the park, but I thought something homemade..."

"Sounds wonderful." She smiled at him, sadness fading under the prospect of sustenance. "And I'm always hungry."

Because she was always running nonstop, and she usually forgot to eat.

But he could take care of her tonight.

He could even take care of her forever... If things were different.

The back of the taxi had that special smell, as if every contagion in the world had gotten together and had a kegger. But Enzo smelled nice. Kimberlyn let herself stay snuggled in the crook of his arm in silence as the world sped past her window.

One magical night—it was the stuff of every woman's fantasies. Carriage ride with a handsome prince, twinkle lights and chocolaty coffee. Best of all was that the revelation that should've been hard for her to take hadn't really been all that hard. At least once the initial shock of disappointment had passed.

As a perfectionist, Kimberlyn never viewed anything other than 100 percent as success. Knowing she had failed to be chosen by Ootaka for his fellowship should've put a damper on things. But somehow Enzo made it all right.

He didn't say anything about it—there was no way for

him to and maintain the silence he was no doubt sworn to—
but he'd still made it all right. Because it was him. Because
she wanted this for him as badly as she'd wanted it for herself. Her struggle to get through her residency wasn't the
only struggle going on. Every single resident struggled to
get through their training. It seemed never-ending when
you were in the trenches.

While they still had several months left in the program
before she'd have to head on to whatever fellowship she
landed, it already seemed as if the hard part was over. The
past couple of months had been so hard and stressful that
it now seemed like a downhill coast. Regular duties. No
killing herself to try to make an impression.

It surprised her how happy she honestly was for him.
She wanted to be able to say it out loud. But this peaceful,
warm bubble he'd built for them the whole evening would
evaporate the instant she said anything. Congratulating
him tomorrow would have to be soon enough. She'd have
to hope for a front-row seat or a blow-by-blow of the action,
if anyone decided to rub his father's nose in it.

The taxi stopped in front of the brownstone and Kimberlyn patted his hand where she held it, getting his attention. The ride in silence had been nice, but if she didn't
say something soon, he'd continue home in the cab, and
who knew what waited for them tomorrow? She wanted
to hang on to this for a little while longer. "Do you want
to come in?"

"Yes." He fished some money from his pocket and
slipped it to the driver through the window, then opened
the door and climbed out.

When he'd helped her from the back of the car it was a
steady jog up the stairs to get into the house.

Neither of them made a move to stop or slow down until
the door to her unit closed behind them.

As the latch caught, Kimberlyn cast off her coat, bag
and boots, and then began helping him, too.

Though unspoken—like so much between them this evening and in the brief time they'd known one another—Enzo shed his outerwear as quickly as she did and reached for her at the same time.

The kiss she'd been waiting for all evening came hard and sweet. No matter the hours spent out in the chilly autumn night, they didn't carry any of the cold in with them. His mouth covered hers and want built in her so swiftly that all dexterity and grace fled. Her fingers fumbled over buttons and as he drove her toward the bed she staggered like a drunk.

In less than a minute all clothes were off and Enzo left her panting on her back, sinking into the plush satiny comforter.

Hungry kisses trailed down her throat and her shoulder, pausing over the scar left by the surgery to repair her shoulder. He looked at it, ran the tip of his finger over the puckered flesh and kissed it.

Her breath caught. What was he doing? Why was he kissing her scars? He hadn't done that before. He had on occasion touched them, but when they had been together before he hadn't even acknowledged them.

She couldn't speak. She could barely breathe. When he made his way to the still-angry scar on her chest, his touch became so reverent tears gathered in the corners of her eyes.

The way her breath caught must have registered as he slid back up over her to look into her eyes, capturing one of her hands and holding it to his chest. "I'm sorry your friend died, but I'm glad the paramedics took you first."

When she opened her eyes again, those remarkable golden-blue eyes were inches from hers. Truth. Acceptance. No blame, but a lot of regret. She couldn't bring herself to ask for answers. Maybe Enzo had the right way of thinking—don't ask the questions if you don't know whether you can handle the answers. Don't ask the questions if knowledge would ruin your peace.

She pushed against his chest until he rolled, and went with him. The first time they'd been together it had been frantic. Parched, cracked earth soaking up an unexpected storm.

And that had been before she'd known she loved him. Kimberlyn couldn't pinpoint when she'd crossed that line, all she knew was that she had. She loved him. That was probably the real clincher in why she wasn't so disappointed about how things had turned out. Confused still, feeling guilty—though not as much as she would've expected—but not so disappointed.

Sliding down his body, she paid back every kiss and lavished an especially long, wet kiss down the underside of his erection, along the length of him.

Deep shuddering breaths had her crawling back up him to pause, knees extended, holding herself just far enough away to share the heat rushing between them.

It was right there on the tip of her tongue to ask him not to wear a condom. Some primal part of her wanted every inch of him bare but knowing what was coming tomorrow and that in a few months they'd be apart... She fished one from the bedside table and worked it onto him with a slow, rolling stroke before taking him inside.

This time she'd make him the mindless one.

Tomorrow would take care of itself. It had to.

CHAPTER TWELVE

UNLIKE THE FIRST time Enzo had been with Kimberlyn, this time as she snuggled up to him and slept he lay awake, staring at the ceiling.

Last night had been thick with realizations, but right now one commanded his thoughts: the idea of similarities he had in common with his father... If Lyons's reasons were anything like his, it made it hard for his hate to burn as bright.

His plan at the outset had been critically flawed, he saw that now. Knowing him and his family—the reason that he'd fought for the fellowship day after day—wouldn't make her weak to him. But knowing her? Knowing what she'd overcome to be there made him weak to her. In reality, probably just knowing her made him soft to her.

He tilted his head to watch her sleeping. The rich chestnut tresses spread over his arm and the white pillow behind her. The fan of her eyelashes against the tan skin that would forever highlight her scars—even more so after they'd faded and lost their color.

The other scars, the ones he'd finally been ready to know, might never fade—the ghost of the friend that haunted her conscience. She hadn't said it, but the glassy look in her eyes had.

He loved her for it.

Making love to Kimberlyn again hadn't been part of

the plan for the evening, but only an idiot wouldn't have seen it coming. A romantic ride in the park, attraction that was eternally off the rails and consequences of the kind of knowledge he'd spent a lifetime avoiding.

Knowing all he knew about her now, he was supposed to find some way to let her go? Depending on who got the fellowship, one of them would have to leave. No new ground had been discovered last night...

Or it had, but it hadn't made things easier. Just more red wires, and he was still waiting for the yellow or the blue to show up. Anything but the steady stream of reds.

The biggest, reddest one was the realization that had come over the shared cup of coffee when she'd given him the last drink... She loved him, too.

His heart skipped and then began to beat really fast.

She loved him, and if he was feeling this weight, she was feeling it more. She'd been feeling it longer, no doubt.

Three weeks ago he still hadn't thought that the fellowship was going to anyone but him. But she'd done what she'd said she would—spent the past couple of weeks busting her butt to change opinions. The fact that Ootaka had used her so much in the past couple of weeks...he really had no idea which way the dominoes would fall.

What he did know was that he wanted Ootaka to pick Kimberlyn. What he didn't know was whether she'd even accept it if she was chosen over him. But she'd worked so hard to get there.

His chest constricted in a way he couldn't breathe through. If he left now, he could fix this. And if he did it right, she'd accept being selected. If she hated him, loyalty wouldn't stand in her way.

Enzo slid out from under her and hurried around the room, gathering up his clothing.

"You're leaving?"

He looked back at her, sitting sleepy and disheveled in her bed, the pink comforter pooled at her waist, breasts high and bare...no attempt made to hide her scars from him now. Streetlights illuminated the room enough to make looking at her hurt.

And he was about to cause another one. *Do it quickly.*

"I didn't intend to sleep with you." He tugged on his shorts and pants, then looked elsewhere. The more he looked at her, the harder it got. "I just wanted to end things on a good note with the carriage ride. Be a good guy before things change tomorrow."

In his peripheral vision he could see her sweet, bleary expression began to shift, sleep confusion replaced by shadows as her chin lowered. That absence of her face made it worse.

He sat in the chair across the room to get his shoes on. If she touched him, she'd feel his heart thundering in his chest. If he got too close, she'd hear the ragged sounds of his breathing. She'd know he was lying.

"That sounds like..." Her voice was soft, but there was a thready quality that made the words so much worse. "You're leaving me?"

"We haven't really been together, so it's not really a breakup."

Yes, it is.

He ignored the voice in his head. "I'm not going to lie, the sex with you is really good." True, in a watered-down version that felt like a lie.

"But that's all it is, Kim. Good sex is hard to resist." *Lies.*

No one called her Kim. Her friends called her Cricket sometimes, everyone at the hospital called her Davis and he frequently called her Mouse...but every real incarnation of her name felt too real for Enzo to say. "You know things would've had to change in a few hours anyway."

"You said that if it wasn't me, you wanted to help me find a new program."

He looked for his other shoe, and anywhere that wasn't

at her. If he had to do this, it would be in the dark, and he would do it as fast as possible and get out.

"Yeah, well, that's the kind of thing you're supposed to say, right? Social niceties that keep civilization running, stuff you don't expect anyone to take you up on." He got his other shoe and crammed his foot into it, stuffing the socks into his pocket because they took too much time to put on and he needed to get the hell out of there.

She pulled the comforter back and stood up, leaving him an unobstructed view of her body in the golden glow of the streetlights. The urge to touch her, to hold her as tight as she always wanted... If he didn't go now, he'd fail. And, more important, he'd fail her.

All the words he couldn't actually say lodged in his throat, strangling him.

"Lock the door when you go, please. I need a shower... I smell your scent all over me."

Her feet ate up the space between the bed and the en suite and she slammed the door behind her.

He stood for what seemed like an eternity, staring at the bathroom door. This was the end.

Or tomorrow would be, after he made sure she got the fellowship.

The shower ran cold for an eternity. Turning on the water before she knew that Enzo had gone had been a mistake. Now she either had to turn it off and listen, which would let him know she was waiting, or go look...and have him catch her looking.

Unless he really was gone.

She opted to stand there with the water running, hoping it would warm up and allow her to salvage some measure of pride. It was better that he believe she had gotten into the shower to get his scent off her as quickly as possible than to think she was so pathetic that even after that display she'd still be in here thinking pretty much only about him.

Even if that's what she was doing.

The water finally turned hot and she adjusted it as hot as she could stand and stepped under the spray. She didn't feel dirty. She felt raw. Exposed. Stupid?

She stayed in the shower, washing away his touch and scent, but all she wanted to do was crawl back into the bed and their sex sheets, and pretend that the date had ended differently.

If she'd understood what his plan had been last night, maybe she could feel a little better. Empathy was a thing she believed all good doctors should have—the ability to put themselves into someone else's shoes and understand them from the inside out. It made it easier to treat someone if you could guess what treatments they would and wouldn't stick with.

But she couldn't figure him out.

He'd gotten the fellowship, that much she felt certain of.

He'd wanted to give her a good night. Okay. Maybe as a way of saying goodbye? But it hadn't been like that. There had been a real connection, tenderness…right up until he'd suddenly sprang from the bed to leave.

Did he think she wouldn't be happy for him? Was this her fault? Had she made him feel guilty by finally feeling as if she could tell him about her accident without the fear that it would be factored into her performance?

Maybe it was pity. Maybe yesterday he'd found out that she was not getting the fellowship, then in the carriage he'd found out she was even more pathetic than he'd originally thought…and the sex had been pity sex.

Three different kinds of body wash to choose from… She put a little of all three distinctly different scents until it merged into one nightmare of fruity floral patchouli. The heady mix may have rid her of the smell of him she'd been wrapped up in before stepping under the water, but it couldn't clean her doubts away as quickly.

Once she'd showered clean, she stepped out, wrapped

a towel around herself and went to curl up on the chaise longue by the window, unable to face the bed.

Three in the morning, and she needed to talk to someone right now.

Sam was out, and he was Enzo's friend and didn't want to be in the middle.

Holly? Well, probably not.

Tessa would probably be asleep right now, or with her man, doing…

"Dang it." She got up long enough to get her phone, dialed Tessa and sank into the lounge again.

"What's wrong?" The man Tessa had moved out of the brownstone to cohabit with answered. No greeting. As doctors, they were all used to being called in the middle of the night for emergencies, and a twinge of guilt pinged her conscience. Did breaking up count as an emergency?

"Hi, Clay. Can I speak to Tessa?"

"Kimberlyn, what's wrong?" Clay repeated. She could hear the growl in his voice.

"Enzo broke up with me and I have to see Ootaka award him the fellowship tomorrow…" Blurting it out like that was even more pathetic.

"I'm sorry, but Tessa needs her sleep."

She tried again. "If you get dumped at three in the morning, you call your support system at three in the morning. And—"

"She's pregnant." His words bit her argument in half. "She needs rest."

"Oh." Not the right reaction. Her eyes burned and she swallowed. It took a second before her stomach settled and she managed, "Congratulations. Good night."

She disconnected and stared at the screen on her phone. The only other person who would listen at this hour and not turn her away even if she cried until she got the hiccups was in Africa with spotty cell service.

Right. She could take care of herself. She had a world-class stiff upper lip, and she had about ten hours to find it.

Grabbing a throw from the back of the chair, she curled into the lounge to try to sleep. Getting her sex sheets off the bed felt like entirely too much effort.

Although Ootaka had a penchant for formality in everything Kimberlyn had witnessed him doing, when he made plans to announce the recipient of his fellowship he simply had people gather in his office.

As soon as she entered, Kimberlyn was aware of exactly where Enzo stood. She tried not to look at him. Nothing good could come from it. His face was already burned into her memory, right along with his style of breakup.

Besides, she looked terrible today. There had been no nonstop crying last night, just a couple of—or a few—short spells and then the stiff upper lip she'd learned so well in her recovery had returned. Unfortunately, puffy eyes and dark circles didn't go away, no matter how stiff your lip was.

She slipped to the back with Tessa and Sam, who had been kind enough to come for emotional support. She'd stand behind the door if she could, but a back corner was as out of the way as she could get. All she needed was dry eyes and a big smile when Enzo's fellowship was announced. Show she was a good sport, and then quietly leave.

Sam had worked out that something was wrong—and as he'd played a part in her going on the carriage ride the night before, he probably knew it was something to do with Enzo. But, true to his word, he didn't ask. Didn't get in the middle. He just hung around by her and Tessa looking extra-brooding.

Enzo didn't look at her. No matter how she held her head, she could see him in her peripheral vision, all attention focused on Ootaka, who had begun his speech. Of course Enzo's attention should be there.

Hers should be, too.

She tried to pick up the thread of whatever the older surgeon was speaking about. Art in medicine, patience, nerves as steady as your hands.

Hah, if he happened to look her way, he'd be extra-glad of the choice he'd made. Her nerves were clearly not steady today.

Strength had been a matter of survival for her recovery, but at least this wasn't something that would require grief counseling. People broke up. It happened all the time. You played sad music, read lots of Emily Dickinson, possibly went to a bar and had questionable sex with someone inappropriate and then ate ice cream. After that, you moved on. There was a grieving process that your loved ones didn't need to shield you from because you had epic holes in your body, and maybe you couldn't handle the added stress...

Tessa grabbed her arm suddenly, focusing her attention on her friend.

As she opened her mouth to question the grab, she noticed that people were turning to look at her and clapping. Including Ootaka. And Enzo.

Tessa whispered, "Smile. Say thank you."

Kimberlyn whispered back, "Did he say my name?" The room swam in her gaze, and suddenly the other side of the room where Ootaka stood looked as if it was fifty feet away rather than ten.

"Yes," Tessa whispered and then slid her hand free of Kimberlyn's arm to flatten against her back and urge her forward.

Smile. Say thank you.

The instruction repeated in her head and she smiled, a big shaky thing, parroted the words she was to say and went to shake Ootaka's hand.

Did he want her to say other things?

People came forward to congratulate her. Other residents. Some with ribbing about the new kid being teacher's pet. She kept smiling and thanking…

Enzo waited until everyone had gone ahead of him, then stepped up to her.

As soon as she lifted her eyes to look at him, tears welled and made her vision swim.

She'd been so sure it was going to be him.

Now that she looked at him dead-on, he looked kind of bad.

Her mouth opened, and through her strangled voice, she whispered, "I'm sorry."

This was why he didn't want to be around her anymore? None of it had made sense before, and, looking at him now, it still didn't make sense.

"Don't be sorry." He held out his hand to shake hers. By rote, she put her hand in his.

Hand-shaking today, yesterday it had been hand-holding.

She knew her hand shook on its own, and when the brief up-down motion had passed, he let go. She looked down, a million miles of nothing to say filling her head.

His hand shook, too.

Most of the other students had trickled out now, only Tessa, Sam and Ootaka remaining.

Was she ever going to understand this man? The math that got her from last night to this morning didn't add up.

This was his home. He'd have to leave his home for one of the other excellent fellowships. And she'd come to a measure of peace at having the fellowship be his. He did deserve it. He'd done it all without his rotten father, he'd done it all for the pride of his family… And she could give that to him. Maybe that was the lesson she should've learned from Janie, how to sacrifice for others.

"Dr. Ootaka…" she said, turning away from Enzo to the surgeon whose admiration they all had been working for. "I can't accept the fellowship. I'm sorry. I don't want it."

"Mouse, no," Enzo barked out, grabbing her arm to spin her around. "You don't turn this down. You deserve it."

"I don't want it."

"Yes, you do. You're just...worried about me. You don't need to worry about me."

She looked closer. The dark circles and somewhat disheveled quality to his hair didn't speak of someone who'd gone home to have a good night's sleep.

If he'd slept poorly, it was his fault. "Shut up. You don't get to tell me what to do or who I get to worry about. You don't get to tell me what to feel. You made your decision to cut ties with me, and I've made my decision to cut ties with West Manhattan Saints." She gave a firm tug to free her elbow from his hand. "After the year is through, I want to move on somewhere else. Somewhere with more trees, somewhere I fit in better."

"You fit in here," he rasped.

Kimberlyn couldn't look at him. She turned to Ootaka and moderated her voice for his benefit. "I'm very sorry, Doctor. Please know I hold you in the highest esteem. I've made mistakes in the past, and people have sacrificed for me. I'm alive today and someone who should be isn't. She sacrificed for me because she loved me. It's my turn to sacrifice for someone...someone else."

She wouldn't say it was someone she loved, and she wouldn't say it was for Enzo. She couldn't make Ootaka choose him. She just believed he'd be the second choice if she dropped out. And his ego would learn to deal with it, since only the five of them had to ever know about it.

"You would not be sacrificing your position for Dr. DellaToro," Ootaka said finally, though he looked somewhat irritated by the whole thing. Indecision was not his favorite thing. Drama was also not his favorite thing.

When she frowned, he pointed to Enzo and ordered, "Tell her, DellaToro."

Enzo plowed a hand through his hair and paced away

then back. "I knew you wouldn't want to be chosen over me if we were together." His skin had gone pale, and he paced away again, this time sitting down.

Realization began to dawn as she watched his face. "You knew I would be chosen and you...you broke up with me because you thought I would be free of those pesky issues of honor and loyalty that way?"

Her words made him sigh, nose wrinkling in distaste as he did so.

"You're an idiot," she announced.

Ootaka made some kind of sound of affirmation but said nothing.

"It's not idiotic. I wanted it for you more than I wanted it for me. So I stepped out, and I thought I'd made sure that you would take the position and get what you deserved. You were supposed to think I was a rotten bastard and get on with your training."

"No. I was right. You're an idiot." She crossed her arms and with a sigh sat down across the room from him.

"Do you still wish to turn the position down, Kimberlyn?" Ootaka had used her first name, which he never did.

She didn't even need to think about it. "I do."

"Mouse..."

They were taking up his office when neither of them were taking the position... She could show all the emotion she wanted to right now. "Did you hear what I said about sacrifice? Do you really think I'd let you sacrifice for me after what I told you about Janie?"

"I did it because *I love you!*" Enzo yelled, standing up as if he was going to hit something—the wall, the furniture.

"Well, I love you too. Idiot!" Kimberlyn yelled back, because it seemed like the thing to do.

Enzo laughed, but the sound that came out was breathy and insubstantial, which fit his thoughts precisely. He knew she loved him, but there was something altogether different about hearing her say the words. Even when the tender words were shouted and capped off by her calling him an idiot.

He'd vowed to break the habit last night, but it was easier when he didn't have any plans to upset—like now. He calmed, sat again and looked at her. "What do we do now?"

The exasperation that had colored her confession became tinged with amusement. "I suppose we'll have to apply for a bunch of other fellowships and see where we can go together. It's only rocket science if it involves having to go to an entirely different planet to a program that will take us both when one of us is an idiot."

Ootaka's long-suffering expression reached out like a tangible slap. They should be wrapping this up for him. He had other things to do. But as chagrined as Ootaka's expression left him feeling, Tessa's and Sam's smiles countered it. "Think we might be able to get a reference from…?" He hooked a thumb in Ootaka's direction but kept his eyes on Kimberlyn.

"Only if you leave my office right now," Ootaka said, shaking his head and going back to his desk. "I have to consider the applications again, and I have a flight tomorrow. I will write your recommendations and email them. Now go."

The tone in his voice said, *Don't stay a single second longer.* As shaking his hand would have taken more than a couple of seconds, Enzo stood, grabbed Kimberlyn's hand and helped her out of the office in one go.

Last night had been hard on her. It'd been hard on him, but it was his fault. She deserved some pampering. Or at least some firm hugging. He needed it anyway.

Outside, pretty much everyone who had been in the room—those who had applied—stood staring at Ootaka's door.

A sea of questions came. They'd heard shouting from the doctors' lounge—which was nearby—and had come to investigate. Turning to Sam and Tessa, Enzo said, "Fill them in?" and still holding Kimberlyn's hand hurried off down the hallway. Her strides were shorter than his, but he couldn't slow down. With the pace he set they were soon out of the hospital and traversed the short distance between the hospital and Central Park, the site of his best-laid plans...

Just inside the park he turned and pressed her against the trunk of a tree where they'd have a little privacy.

He couldn't name what he saw in her eyes. Love, yes. A bit of fear, though, still. As sure as her words had been, he had to make her say it one more time. "Tell me one more time that you're sure."

"I'm sure that I love you." In the sunlight, he could see the hint of redness still clinging to her eyes. He'd definitely made her cry last night. And maybe this morning, too. After a long look into his eyes, she added, "And I'm sure that I want to be with you. I just have a few requirements."

Though pretty certain he knew what she was going to say, Enzo asked the question. "Lay them on me."

She cupped his cheeks and held his head where she could look into his eyes. "I want to know when you came up with that harebrained scheme?"

"While you were asleep."

"After the romantic carriage ride, picnic, conversation and sex?"

He nodded, though it was the last thing he wanted to admit to. "I panicked. Didn't know what else to do."

"Talk. For future reference, the solution is to talk." Her thumbs stroked his cheeks and she leaned up to kiss him. "About anything, everything. No forbidden topics. Got it?"

He nodded again, tilting his forehead against hers, his hands sliding up the back of her scrub top. "I also had another thought last night. When we were in the carriage. Before you told me about Janie... I never really put a reason to why I didn't want to know about the extent of your surgeries, but it was because I didn't want my thinking about you to be forced to change. I was comfortable with the facts that I knew."

He gave her a minute to absorb his words, but when she still looked confused he explained. "I learned it from Lyons. With all that I thought I'd learned from Ernst about how to love someone—family, friends—I never unlearned that first lesson. Lyons stopped asking about us. All communication with Mom stopped not long after he left. He didn't want to know anything. I don't really know his reasons for that, but I think I understand. I didn't want to know anything that would jeopardize my plans, and I think it would've worked if I could've just stopped asking questions. The more I knew you, the more I needed to know. If I were Lyons, if I felt like I needed out for some reason, I'm pretty sure it would've been with an all-or-nothing mindset. Not that I think I could do that with someone I loved, maybe he's just not as evolved as I am."

The smile that came went a long way to settling his nerves. "So, what if his offer was an olive branch? How does that idea change your plans?"

"I texted him this morning while I was waiting for Ootaka to show up."

For all that the morning had felt like running on shifting sand, that confession rocked Kimberlyn the hardest. Though his arms were around her, she wanted a hand to hold and slipped her arm around to grab one of his so she could link their fingers. "What did you text? Did he answer?"

"I told him that if something had changed, that if he wanted to get to know us, he should start with Maya. His granddaughter could be his clean slate, and we'd see where it went from there. Gave him information about her birthday coming up, sent a picture I had on my phone..."

"You had a busy morning," she whispered. It was like having a hope-filled prognosis for a terminal patient, that miracle she'd wanted for Mr. Elliot. "What did he say?"

"He said she has his mother's eyes."

Maya had Enzo's eyes. And Sophia's, and their father's... "Is he going to see her?"

"Sophia's going to let me take her to his house to visit. She's not ready to go there, and I think we should start small anyway... So, maybe you and I can take her there together?"

Kimberlyn nodded, not trusting herself to say anything right now. It wasn't a cure, but it was a treatment full of promise.

Enzo leaned his forehead against hers and added, "I'd really like to talk about going home now. Being alone with you. We have some other decisions to make, but I'm so tired..."

He'd still sacrificed for her, but she'd sacrificed for him right back. Everything was in the air, uncertain, at least when it came to where they'd be in six months. But at the center of all the uncertainty she could feel a rock rising. Wherever they ended up, they'd finish this together. They'd be together.

But that didn't mean she couldn't torture him a little bit first. "I don't know if I can invite you back after all these emotional displays." She found her smile, her damp eyes rapidly drying. "I might have to make you pay for all this drama."

"In orgasms?" The rascally smile returned, and the tenderness in his eyes made a perfect match for it.

"I haven't decided yet."

"Just so you know, it's a debt I intend to make good on." He pulled her away from the tree and steered her back toward the street for a cab, and home.

EPILOGUE

BRADFORD PEARS BLOOMED up and down the street in front of the Brooklyn brownstone. Kimberlyn paused after placing yet another box into the back of the moving truck, just to get a good look at the few white, puffy trees she could see.

"Are they talking to you?" Enzo asked, after loading what he carried of Caren's furniture into the back.

Kimberlyn looked over her shoulder as he came behind her, arms slipping around her waist. "The trees?"

"Is it going to rain or anything?" Enzo rested his chin against the bare skin on her shoulder. The scar there had faded enough for her to feel comfortable going sleeveless. First the shoulder, then maybe the thigh this summer when it became shorts weather. Every day they got a little lighter, and her guilt went along with it.

"Not that I can tell. You need green leaves for that." She leaned fully against him, linking her fingers with his—after a small pause to right the seat of the diamond ring on her finger. One day, after the fellowship was done and there was a matching wedding band to hold it steady, maybe it would stop turning like that. "I will teach you all about the weather-forecasting properties of trees once we get to Tennessee—where it's warmer and the trees will have green on them."

Caren had decided to extend her mission to Cameroon for another year, which left Kimberlyn and Enzo to pack the apartment and move her things back home. No one knew how long she intended to stay, or whether she'd return to New York when she came back to the United States.

Kimberlyn understood: Caren had found something worth fighting for, and she prayed every day that it turned out to be even half as good as what she'd found with Enzo. Grief healed more slowly than the body, and though every day Kimberlyn got a little bit better, there were certain promises she couldn't budge on.

She would become the best trauma surgeon she could be, even if that wasn't the world's best trauma surgeon. That detail wasn't within her control.

She would finish her training and establish her practice before she got married. Enzo had said he could live with a two-year engagement, and he'd stopped saying the wedding was just a formality anyway...because that jeopardized the letter of her promise. Because grief, and the heart, healed more slowly than the body.

"Okay. There's a couple more boxes, and my mom called—she packed up an unholy amount of food for the road. I think it's a ploy to make us swing by and say goodbye again."

"Did you tell her that we'll come back for the holidays and that anytime she wants to come stay we'd love to see her?"

"I told her." He kissed her neck and let go to dash back up the stairs into the house.

They'd given the same invitation to Marcus Lyons, though no one was at that point of comfort yet. He might visit, but he'd stay at a hotel if he came. It was progress.

Tennessee wasn't so far away. New York had just felt like another planet when she'd first got there. Enzo would get used to it there, and two years wasn't so long if he wanted to move back up north when they'd finished their fellowship at Vanderbilt.

Because being mentored by one of Ootaka's fellows

was the very next best thing to being mentored by Oo-taka himself.

And there was nothing better than being where she was right now, and there could never be anything better than being loved by Enzo.

Though she might change her mind in two years, when they could talk about a little cousin for Maya...

* * * * *

Don't miss the next story in the fabulous
NEW YORK CITY DOCS *series*
FALLING AT THE SURGEON'S FEET
by Lucy Ryder
Available September 2015!

MILLS & BOON®
Hardback – August 2015

ROMANCE

The Greek Demands His Heir	Lynne Graham
The Sinner's Marriage Redemption	Annie West
His Sicilian Cinderella	Carol Marinelli
Captivated by the Greek	Julia James
The Perfect Cazorla Wife	Michelle Smart
Claimed for His Duty	Tara Pammi
The Marakaios Baby	Kate Hewitt
Billionaire's Ultimate Acquisition	Melanie Milburne
Return of the Italian Tycoon	Jennifer Faye
His Unforgettable Fiancée	Teresa Carpenter
Hired by the Brooding Billionaire	Kandy Shepherd
A Will, a Wish...a Proposal	Jessica Gilmore
Hot Doc from Her Past	Tina Beckett
Surgeons, Rivals...Lovers	Amalie Berlin
Best Friend to Perfect Bride	Jennifer Taylor
Resisting Her Rebel Doc	Joanna Neil
A Baby to Bind Them	Susanne Hampton
Doctor...to Duchess?	Annie O'Neil
Second Chance with the Billionaire	Janice Maynard
Having Her Boss's Baby	Maureen Child

MILLS & BOON®
Large Print – August 2015

ROMANCE

The Billionaire's Bridal Bargain	Lynne Graham
At the Brazilian's Command	Susan Stephens
Carrying the Greek's Heir	Sharon Kendrick
The Sheikh's Princess Bride	Annie West
His Diamond of Convenience	Maisey Yates
Olivero's Outrageous Proposal	Kate Walker
The Italian's Deal for I Do	Jennifer Hayward
The Millionaire and the Maid	Michelle Douglas
Expecting the Earl's Baby	Jessica Gilmore
Best Man for the Bridesmaid	Jennifer Faye
It Started at a Wedding...	Kate Hardy

HISTORICAL

A Ring from a Marquess	Christine Merrill
Bound by Duty	Diane Gaston
From Wallflower to Countess	Janice Preston
Stolen by the Highlander	Terri Brisbin
Enslaved by the Viking	Harper St. George

MEDICAL

A Date with Her Valentine Doc	Melanie Milburne
It Happened in Paris...	Robin Gianna
The Sheikh Doctor's Bride	Meredith Webber
Temptation in Paradise	Joanna Neil
A Baby to Heal Their Hearts	Kate Hardy
The Surgeon's Baby Secret	Amber McKenzie

MILLS & BOON®
Hardback – September 2015

ROMANCE

The Greek Commands His Mistress	Lynne Graham
A Pawn in the Playboy's Game	Cathy Williams
Bound to the Warrior King	Maisey Yates
Her Nine Month Confession	Kim Lawrence
Traded to the Desert Sheikh	Caitlin Crews
A Bride Worth Millions	Chantelle Shaw
Vows of Revenge	Dani Collins
From One Night to Wife	Rachael Thomas
Reunited by a Baby Secret	Michelle Douglas
A Wedding for the Greek Tycoon	Rebecca Winters
Beauty & Her Billionaire Boss	Barbara Wallace
Newborn on Her Doorstep	Ellie Darkins
Falling at the Surgeon's Feet	Lucy Ryder
One Night in New York	Amy Ruttan
Daredevil, Doctor...Husband?	Alison Roberts
The Doctor She'd Never Forget	Annie Claydon
Reunited...in Paris!	Sue MacKay
French Fling to Forever	Karin Baine
Claimed	Tracy Wolff
Maid for a Magnate	Jules Bennett

MILLS & BOON®
Large Print – September 2015

ROMANCE

The Sheikh's Secret Babies	Lynne Graham
The Sins of Sebastian Rey-Defoe	Kim Lawrence
At Her Boss's Pleasure	Cathy Williams
Captive of Kadar	Trish Morey
The Marakaios Marriage	Kate Hewitt
Craving Her Enemy's Touch	Rachael Thomas
The Greek's Pregnant Bride	Michelle Smart
The Pregnancy Secret	Cara Colter
A Bride for the Runaway Groom	Scarlet Wilson
The Wedding Planner and the CEO	Alison Roberts
Bound by a Baby Bump	Ellie Darkins

HISTORICAL

A Lady for Lord Randall	Sarah Mallory
The Husband Season	Mary Nichols
The Rake to Reveal Her	Julia Justiss
A Dance with Danger	Jeannie Lin
Lucy Lane and the Lieutenant	Helen Dickson

MEDICAL

Baby Twins to Bind Them	Carol Marinelli
The Firefighter to Heal Her Heart	Annie O'Neil
Tortured by Her Touch	Dianne Drake
It Happened in Vegas	Amy Ruttan
The Family She Needs	Sue MacKay
A Father for Poppy	Abigail Gordon